W9-AOI-433

A Telling
of the Tales

A Telling of the Tales

FIVE STORIES

William J. Brooke

Drawings by Richard Egielski

HarperTrophy
A Division of HarperCollins*Publishers*

A Telling of the Tales: Five Stories
Text copyright © 1990 by William J. Brooke
Illustrations copyright © 1990 by Richard Egielski
Printed in the U.S.A. All rights reserved.
Typography by Al Cetta

Library of Congress Cataloging-in-Publication Data
Brooke, William J.
   A telling of the tales : five stories / by William J. Brooke.
      p.   cm.
   Summary: A retelling of five classic folk/fairy tales, including
Cinderella, Sleeping Beauty, Paul Bunyan, John Henry, and Jack and the
Beanstalk, from a contemporary perspective.
   ISBN 0-06-020688-8. — ISBN 0-06-020689-6 (lib. bdg.)
   ISBN 0-06-440467-6 (pbk.)
   1. Children's stories, American. [1. Short stories.] I. Egielski,
Richard, ill. II. Title.
PZ7.B78977Te   1990   89-36588
[Fic]—dc20   CIP
                                                             AC

First Harper Trophy edition, 1993.

With love and gratitude
to
Colby, Katie and Keith
for Opera Camp August 1988
and to
Lynne
for once and ever after

Contents

The telling of a tale links you with everyone who has told it before. There are no new tales, only new tellers, telling in their own way, and if you listen closely you can hear the voice of everyone who ever told the tale.

—from "The Telling of a Tale"

The Waking of the Prince

DUCKING UNDER A GOUT of flame, the Prince threw himself forward into a double roll and with the last of his strength thrust the sword upward into the soft underbelly of the dragon. He staggered back from the blast of steam and blood that boiled forth as the creature sank to the ground. When the mists cleared, the dragon had crumbled into dust, the forest of thorns had melted into the ground, and a newly bright sun shone down upon castle and countryside.

The Prince took a moment to thrill at the adventure of it all. Then he spun and charged beneath the portcullis, into the gloom of the staircase spiraling up into the tower. He ignored the sleeping forms that made the castle grounds seem a bloodless battlefield. Up and up through the last twist into the topmost chamber where, facedown before a simple spinning wheel, lay a still, feminine figure in regal attire.

Willing his heart to still its pounding, the Prince gently turned her over and gasped.

Here was beauty beyond beauty! Her hair was deep brown, almost black, like the last of twilight yielding to night, a starry night shot through with many a dancing gleam. Her face was a snowfield reflecting moonlight amid that star-shot night, each feature precisely etched, yet soft and glowing as if from within. Her mouth lolled slightly open in the sweet abandon of her childlike sleep, so totally helpless and trusting that a man might happily give his life to protect that slumber that the Prince was about to end.

He drank her in for a moment, then leaned forward and pressed his lips to hers. Never was there such a kiss! In his mind he could hear the echo of this moment in the songs of all ages to come.

He felt warmth awaken in her mouth and saw color rushing to the curve of her cheeks. Her eyes fluttered and opened, and his heart was lost in those deep-green pools set in alabaster and arched over with ebony.

She looked at him in dreamy confusion as he spoke.

"I am Prince Valorian. I have won my way past the forest of thorns and the evil fairy who guarded your bower in dragon shape to awaken you from your hundred-year slumber."

Her eyes came into sharper focus. She seemed to really see him then. She spoke and her voice was music.

"Do you have any form of identification with you?" she asked.

"Identification?"

"Well, you don't look particularly like a Prince. Your clothes are a mess."

"I had some little difficulty in getting here, as I said."

"Where are my guards? They should be here. Particularly today. It's my twenty-first birthday and I'm supposed to be extra careful. . . . I don't mean to be rude, but I shouldn't be talking to strange men today."

"It's not your twenty-first birthday, actually," the Prince said, a little put out. "It's your hundred-and-twenty-first."

She looked at him a moment, then tried a sincere smile, which didn't work. "You didn't happen to notice any guards on your way up, did you?"

"Yes, but they're all asleep, or just beginning to wake up, I suppose. Listen to me—you've been asleep for a hundred years. I have just awakened you."

Her smile grew brittle. "No, that's what I'm supposed to be on guard against, a curse or something. I had to stay away from spinning wheels until my twenty-first birthday."

The Prince gestured to the wheel. "Didn't quite make it, did you?"

"Well, I found this one and touched it and I guess I was so nervous that I fainted for a moment, but now I'm fine."

The Prince sighed with some exasperation. This was not working out as he had expected.

"The curse worked," he said shortly. "You slept a hundred years. The whole kingdom slept a hundred years. A forest of thorns grew up. A dragon guarded the entry. I fought my way through. I awakened you. And here we are."

She smiled again in that way that was beginning to irritate him. "Did you say you had some identification? Just out of curiosity?"

He held out his hand. "My signet ring."

She scrutinized it. "Very attractive. I don't seem to recognize the seal."

"I am Prince Valorian of Swederbaum, the son of Silarion, the grandson of Hilarion."

"Swederbaum," she mused. "I don't know it."

"Well, there *have* been some changes in the old neighborhood in the last hundred years."

There was a clatter on the stairs, and a great panting and puffing, and twelve armed guards finally rushed into the room. The Captain knelt at the Princess's feet and began, "Your Highness, I am deeply sorry we were not with you, but . . ." Suddenly his eyes went round. He spun to his men and screamed, "Attack!"

They leaped fearlessly at the spinning wheel and

[6]

wrestled it to the ground, tangling themselves considerably in the wool. The Captain stood between the Princess and the battle with sword drawn to protect her, presumably against any sudden moves by the spinning wheel.

At last the tangle of men made its way to a window, and the wheel was hurled out. The Captain turned and saluted smartly, clapping his sword hilt to his forehead. "All clear!" he shouted. "The room is secured."

"Thank you, Captain," the Princess said sweetly. "Now could you please find my father, the King, and tell him that I wish to see him."

"At once, Your Highness. Fall in! Right face! Double time! One, two, three, four!" The twelve men struggled themselves into some order and started to rush out.

"One of you!" the Princess called. "One of you can take the message. The others should stay and . . ." She glanced sideways at the Prince, then finished innocently, ". . . keep an eye out for any possible trouble."

"Shmendrick!" the Captain bellowed. One of the guards untangled from his fellows and stepped forward, saluted, missed, and struck the man behind him. "Double time! To the King! Tell him . . ." But Shmendrick was already out of the room and racing down the stairs.

"Tell him his daughter is in good hands and wants to see him!" the Captain shouted.

There were the sounds of metal crashing repeatedly against wood and stone, then "Good hands" and "See him" echoed weakly upward.

"A farce," thought the Prince. "I am a hero trapped in a comedy."

"Captain," said the Princess.

"Your Highness!" snapped the Captain.

"Have you or any of your men," she began, glancing slyly at the Prince, "been sleeping lately?"

Among the guards, eyes widened and sweat started. Furtive glances were cast and avoided. "You mean since we came on duty?"

"Yes, Captain."

"Certainly not, Your Highness! Right, men?" Elaborate pantomimes of innocence. "May I ask who has been spreading such unwarranted rumors about us?"

"Oh, no one of any importance, Captain. Tell me," and now she was grinning sarcastically at the Prince, "did you and your men see the forest of thorns?"

"Forest of thorns?" The Captain and his men looked at each other, trying to decide if this was some form of subtle accusation.

"Yes, it's all over the castle, I've heard."

"*Was* all over the castle," the Prince tried to correct her, but he couldn't be heard for the clatter of the guards rushing to the windows to see this wonderful sight.

"And, of course, the dragon," the Princess concluded, grinning triumphantly.

"Dragon?" the Captain gulped, as his men froze.

"Yes, at the gates. Big and fire breathing, I assume?" She raised eyebrows at the Prince, but he declined to confirm.

The men at the windows were suddenly cured of all curiosity, having acquired instead a sudden intense interest in the center of the room.

The Princess strolled to the window and idly glanced out. "No, no dragons in sight, no forest of thorns. I must have been misinformed."

The Prince was beginning to regret the whole episode. Still, she *was* quite beautiful and he owed it to himself to establish his own position in this adventure. "I slew the dragon. The forest of thorns melted away."

"And why did you do that?"

"So that I could awaken you. The whole world knows your story, the beauty sleeping in the tower, unreachable, unattainable. I had to see you for myself and become a part of this greatest adventure of all."

The Princess was not displeased by this answer. She twirled a lock of hair playfully around one finger, dark silky threads on an ivory bobbin. "And how did you wake me from my hundred-year catnap? Did you crow like a cock or did you toss pebbles at my window?"

"I kissed you."

For a moment she was silent, but her mouth dropped open into a perfect O. Her cheeks flushed most becomingly. She stepped close and looked up into his face. She raised one dainty hand toward his cheek. Her eyelids drooped and her head tilted back. The Prince smiled down at her, pleased that she was finally appreciating him. He just had time to notice her hand accelerating before it slapped his face with surprising force.

"Kissed me," she said, turning coldly away. "Did it occur to you that I might not wish to be kissed?"

The Prince rubbed his chin in surprise. "No, it didn't. I just made the assumption that a young, beautiful, vibrant Princess would also like to include consciousness among her attributes."

The Princess softened a bit at the adjectives, but retained her haughtiness. "I have read of many entirely satisfactory rulers who never demonstrated any overt signs of consciousness at all."

"I can't believe you would be like that. For you, the world should blossom anew each morning. Every day should be an adventure waiting to unfold."

The Princess was pensive and the Prince thought again how nice she looked when she wasn't being thoroughly unpleasant. "Adventure," she mused. "Adventure is what happens in stories, not in real life. Real life is dressing properly and needlepoint and preparing myself to be a suitable consort."

The Prince smiled ruefully at that, and she noticed he had a very nice smile.

"You have slept," he said, "even longer than I thought. I have come just in time. The world lies open before us! Pack a bag! We'll be off by nightfall!"

"Off where?"

"To the mountains where dawn awakens! To the land where men grow tails and women spin gold! To the home of the cyclops and the haunt of the basilisk! Wherever fancy and the four winds take us!"

For a moment, a light glowed in her eyes, then she blinked and recovered. "Captain!" she snapped.

The guardsmen had been pretending not to listen, while maneuvering as close as possible. The Captain now clanged a salute from just behind the Princess that made her jump.

"Arrest this man," she instructed him, turning away with a show of indifference.

The Captain raised his sword and stepped toward the Prince. "Sirrah, I command you to yield yourself to my sword." He held the point to the Prince's breast.

"This sword?" the Prince asked, grabbing the flat of the blade, jerking the Captain forward, striking his forearm, twisting the sword away and throwing it out the window.

The Captain rubbed his arm and stared out the window. A distant clang echoed up from the courtyard. "Well, that was the one I had in mind."

"Go get it and I'll consider yielding to it."

The Captain started for the stairs . . . then shook his head and ordered his men, "Seize him!"

Before they could move, the Prince slammed one man against the wall, jerked his sword from his scabbard, and threw it out the window. Another man drew, and the Prince spun him to the window, rapped his wrist on the sill, and sent his blade to join the others. Turning, striking, twisting, the Prince made quick work of most of the guards, then stood out of the way so the last three could get to the window to throw their swords out in a gesture of friendship and conciliation.

The Prince stood, arms folded, facing the Princess. He was breathing slightly heavier than before, but his smile was much broader. This was more like it! "I hope," he said, "the Princess will reconsider her order and offer me better hospitality."

The Princess drew herself up. "Perhaps I was hasty," she said at last. "May I offer you the hospitality of this chamber until my father arrives."

The Prince looked around the bare room. "Since you offer so graciously, how can I refuse?"

"Captain," said the Princess. There was a movement, which might have been an attempted salute, near the bottom of a pile of bodies. "I rescind my order. This gentleman is not to be bothered."

"If Your Highness wishes," a muffled voice responded.

The Prince leaned against the wall while the Princess feigned nonchalance at the window. The guards stood up and arranged themselves as close to the stairs as possible.

After a few moments of silence, the Prince started

3. Mrs. Hubbard drew Poirot a little aside.

"You know, I'm dead scared of that man. Oh! not the v[...]
There's something *wrong* about that man. My daug[...]
Mamma gets a hunch, she's dead right,' that's what n[...]
that man. He's next door to me and I don't like it. I pu[...]
last night. I thought I heard him trying the handle. D[...]
that man turned out to be a murderer—one of these [...]

(Part I, chapter 4)

Recognizing foreshadowing: As you read the next few ch[...]
Below, record an example. Be prepared to explain what t[...]
future.

_____

_____

_____

_____

_____

_____

_____

© COPYRIGHT, The Center for Learning. Use[...]

to say ironically, "Lovely weather we're . . ." The Princess stamped her foot and turned on him.

"No!" she blurted, "I will not listen to the weather! When a man talks about the weather to a woman it is because he thinks her incapable of understanding anything else." Her eyes burned with an emerald fire.

The Prince bowed slightly. "I would never so insult you, but when I speak of *you*, you strike me, and when I speak of *me*, you order me arrested. The weather seemed the only safe subject." The Princess smiled slightly, so he hurried on. "If I could speak my mind, I would say that your eyes are the most beautiful I have ever . . ."

"I know flattery when I hear it." The Princess smiled at him.

"Then you also know truth," he replied, smiling in turn.

And suddenly that sleeping softness returned to her face as she asked, "Has your life been filled with adventures?" And though her face was gentle, her eyes fixed his with a strength he could not master, and he was drawn down into their depths, into a hollow place he couldn't fathom. How lucky a man might be, he thought, if he could only find the thing to fill that void. Or *be* the thing himself.

Before he could find breath to answer, there was a sound of feet upon the stairs, then the sound of wheezing. A voice echoed up, "I'm coming, my dear, just a moment more, I'll be there, oh, my goodness."

"Papa is not as young as he used to be," the Princess said, and turned her eyes away from the Prince.

"By a hundred years," the Prince agreed. The Princess gave a little sniff, and her look turned from snow and ocean depth back to alabaster and jade.

At last a florid face framed in bushy side-whiskers and crowned with snow-white hair and a golden coronet appeared above the edge of the stairwell. "My dear? Are you all right?"

She hurried to help him up the last few stairs. "I'm fine, Daddy, but what took you so long?"

"We would have been here sooner, but it was raining swords in the courtyard."

The Prince bowed civilly to the King. "Your Majesty."

"Who's this?" the King whispered loudly to his daughter.

"This man claims to be a Prince. He broke into the castle, he resisted arrest and . . ."

"Slew the dragon," interjected the Prince, "melted the forest of thorns, awakened the Princess and the populace from their enchanted sleep . . ."

"And kissed me!" the Princess finished decisively.

The King stared, befuddled. Finally, he spoke to the Prince.

"Do you happen to have any form of identification?"

The Prince's brow knit and he stamped his foot. "What is this insistence upon who I am?" he stormed.

"A man is what he does! Judge me by my deeds, not by my name! Forgive my ill temper, Your Majesty, but it has been a long day."

He then repeated his whole story to the King, while the Princess stared out the window and snorted occasionally to show her disdain. But in fact she was listening with some care.

When the Prince was finished, the Princess said, "You see, Father, this ridiculous man is . . ."

"Now, daughter," he said soothingly, "we mustn't be impolite. In fact, what he describes is exactly what we were warned might happen. However," he addressed the Prince, "our difficulty is that there is no proof of what you say. One would certainly think that a hundred-year sleep would leave some kind of evidence."

"Well, if Your Majesty would just confer with my father, Silarion of Swederbaum, he can confirm . . ."

"No, no, if there has been some sort of disruption in the neighboring kingdoms, I don't think we can take their word for what might have happened. This could be a plot to usurp our power, after all. Tell me, what is it you wanted in coming here?"

The Prince was taken aback. "Well, the idea was that the Princess would, well, love me and—"

"Love you!" the Princess exploded. "Of all the conceited . . ."

"Love me and we would marry and live hap—"

"Father! Are you going to let this man talk of . . ."

"Now, Daughter, if he is a Prince and if he has done all he says and if you really slept a hundred years, then . . ." He paused in thought.

"Then what?"

"I'm not sure."

"If he really awakened me from a hundred-year sleep with a kiss, wouldn't I have fallen in love with him on the spot? That's what happens in stories. It seems to me that would be part of the enchantment."

"Me, too," said the Prince. There was a clatter of mail and metal as the guards nodded their agreement.

"Well, I *didn't* fall in love with him. In fact, I don't like him at all," the Princess insisted stubbornly.

The King turned to the Prince. "What are your feelings toward my daughter?"

The Prince thought. "I guess I love her. I have thought about her for so long and I have gone through so many hardships to win her. Yes, I love her. Of course I love her! That is part of the adventure!"

The Princess started to respond to that, but the King silenced her with a look. "I think the only thing to do is ask for some proof of your love. You must perform a heroic deed." He stopped the Prince's protest. "I know, I know, you already have, but we don't have any proof of that. Humor us."

After a moment's struggle with himself, the Prince asked, "What sort of deed?"

[16]

"Oh, a dragon would be acceptable, I think. That's sort of standard."

"I just slew the only dragon I know of!"

"That was an evil fairy masquerading as a dragon, according to your story, so I don't think it counts. Now there is a very famous dragon in the kingdom of Farflungia that would fit the bill nicely. Ignispirus Magnus is his name."

"I've never heard of him," the Prince said. "He must have died in the last hundred years."

"Well, I'm sure you'll find him if you look carefully. Now bring us back his head and we'll talk some more. If you've really done all you claim, this will be child's play."

The Prince strode thoughtfully to the stairs, the guards giving way before him. He stopped and looked at the Princess, who refused to return his look but flushed very prettily at his attention.

"Actually, after the events of the last hour, fighting a dragon might be a pleasant change." He proceeded down the stairs.

There was silence for a moment, then the King cleared his throat in the dry little way he always did when he was about to start on one of his father-daughter talks that were meant to be firm but were in fact extremely timid.

The Princess swept out before he could get started. "I'm tired," she announced. "I'm going to take a nap."

The King was left to sigh and stare out the window at his domain, and to wonder why it was easier to rule a kingdom than a daughter.

———

Ducking under a gout of flame, the Prince threw himself forward into a double roll and with the last of his strength thrust the sword upward into the soft underbelly of the dragon.

Or, rather, what *should* have been the soft underbelly of the dragon, but was in fact empty space. The dragon looked down at him from where it hovered, wings flapping, just a foot out of reach.

"Nice moves," it said, its throaty rasp making it hard to tell if sarcasm was intended.

Swinging his arm in a wide circle, the Prince quickly released the sword, hurling it upward into the soft underbelly of the, well, no, what *should* have been the soft underbelly of the dragon. The sword arced upward through empty space, where a twisted claw plucked it neatly from the air and added it to the cascading pile of treasure in the corner.

The Prince feinted toward the cave entrance, then threw himself on the treasure heap and scrambled upward toward his sword. He felt a tug at the back of his neck, an upward rush, and found his feet churning a lot of nothing.

"This is not going well," he thought. Out loud, he said, "Give me back my sword," but a flick of a claw sent him sprawling into a tight corner, where the dragon settled in front of him. The Prince watched in dismay as the dragon drew itself up to tower over him. He saw the great body expand, then the swelling of the neck as what he assumed was the flame for his funeral pyre rushed up the throat.

"You can keep the sword!" he shouted as the great jaws gaped open before him.

He was surrounded by a terrible rush of hot air, and the ground shook. He closed his eyes and tried to think of the Princess in what was probably his last moment. Somehow, he could not conjure up her face. He could remember all the stories and he could remember the years of thinking about her, but he could not quite picture her face.

He had been wondering about this for a while when he noticed that he was still alive and not even particularly warm. He opened his eyes. The dragon was looking at him from behind one of its stubby wings and fluttering the wiry lashes of its bug eyes. If the green face could have turned red, he would have described it as embarrassed.

"Excuse me," the dragon rasped.

"What happened?" the Prince managed to get out.

The dragon looked away. "Heartburn. I'm sorry. I'm not used to this kind of activity." It rose into the air again and settled atop its treasure. The Prince found that his knees were more than a little shaky and seated himself on a rock.

"Not that it wasn't fun," the dragon added. "Haven't

had a good set-to in decades. That double roll of yours is especially picturesque."

"I killed a dragon with it just recently, as a matter of fact," the Prince said defensively, before realizing that might not be a very polite thing to say. But the dragon took no offense.

"Must have been a young one."

"Well," the Prince allowed, "it was really an evil fairy masquerading as a dragon."

"Ah." The dragon breathed happily, settling back and scrunching down into its treasure comfortably. "You don't live long as a dragon without learning to cover your belly."

"How old *are* you?" Now that his shock was over, the Prince was sidling toward the entrance, trying to cover his movement with polite conversation.

"About three hundred years, as you reckon it. I used to be the terror of three kingdoms, stealing maidens, burning villages, you name it." The dragon sat up suddenly and fixed the Prince with its gaze, stopping his progress toward the exit. "I'm being thoughtless, aren't I? You must be upset by my mention of such things. It's just that I have so little company, I've lost all sense of good manners."

"No, not at all. I'm rather interested in such things, adventures and so forth."

"Yes," the dragon mused, settling back again, "you're young, aren't you? Sometimes it's hard to tell, humans look so much alike. But, then, who else but a youngster would make the effort to try to slay an old has-been like me?"

The Prince reached the cave entrance and ran out as fast as he could.

"Wait!" the dragon wailed behind him. "Don't go!"

The Prince concealed himself behind some rocks just as the grisly head on its snaky neck thrust out from the cave. The big eyes turned in every direction, then the lids lowered in disappointment.

"I was going to make us tea," the dragon said.

————

The Princess leaned back from her needlepoint and sighed.

The Queen looked at her with a measuring eye. It was one of her best expressions.

"Thinking of that young Prince again, I expect. You and your father might have had the courtesy to introduce him to me."

"I was not thinking *of* him," the Princess said. When the Queen continued to scrutinize her, she admitted, "I was thinking *about* him. There is a great difference!" she finished.

The Queen gave a little "Hem!" just to show that there was much she could have said on the subject if she wished, then asked, "What were you thinking *about* the young Prince, then?" Her hands did not pause in their turning of an embroidery hoop, passing the needle from one side to the other.

The Princess gestured at the screen before her.

"Here we sit, creating scenes of chivalry, unicorns, dragons, deeds of valor. And there he is out there living those same scenes. It doesn't seem fair."

The Queen pursed her lips in consideration. "No, I daresay it isn't fair, but I'm sure he has learned to live with it."

The Princess blinked twice. "I mean it isn't fair to *us*!"

The Queen blinked three times. "What an extraordinary idea! Do you really think you'd rather be out there facing hardship and danger than tucked up cozy here by the fire?"

"Of course I'd prefer that! Oh, my life is so boring!" She paced back and forth before the mantel. "I sit and sew, I practice on the lute, I wave to the people from the balcony . . ."

"You dress magnificently, you eat splendidly, some-day you will be given in marriage to a great family . . ."

"And then I'll get to watch my sons go off to adventures and I'll raise my daughters to be as dull as I am."

The Queen clicked her tongue to show that that did not deserve comment. "If what this Prince says is correct," she said, "you've already had your great adventure."

"And I slept all the way through it." The Princess stared into the fire. "I wish . . ." she whispered.

"That you were with him?" the Queen inquired,

arching her eyebrows and lowering her eyelids. It was a difficult expression, but she practiced it mornings in the looking glass.

"That I *was* him," the Princess whispered to herself expressionlessly.

―――

"Oh, Ignispirus!" the Prince warbled in what he hoped was a conciliatory tone.

There was silence from the cave mouth.

"Yoo hoo, Ignispirus!"

Still nothing.

"Iggy!"

There was a burst of flame closely followed by a huge green head with flashing eyes.

"Unauthorized nicknames are exceedingly rude!"

"I'm deeply sorry," the Prince said. "I came here to apologize for yesterday."

"Apologize?" The dragon curled its neck into a great S, for "suspicion," perhaps.

"For leaving so abruptly. I want to apologize and take you up on your offer of tea." He froze as the great face dropped down and an eyeball bigger than his head glared into his eyes from a foot away.

"And why *did* you leave so abruptly?" This close, the Prince could feel the dragon's voice vibrating in all the hollow spaces of his own body.

It took several efforts to get it out, but finally the Prince sputtered, "I was somewhat concerned . . ."

"Concerned?"

"A little nervous . . ."

"Nervous?"

A deep breath. "I was frightened out of my wits."

The dragon laughed at that.

The Prince was a bit annoyed. "After all, you are a fire-breathing dragon. It's no sign of weakness to experience a little natural . . ."

"But I didn't hurt you a bit. I was very careful not to hurt you. I could have, you know"—it winked coyly—"but I didn't. Why do people insist on thinking that just because one is a dragon . . ."

"You told me yourself you had pillaged and burned."

"Mere childish shenanigans."

"You shot fire at me!"

"Because you came in here swinging that sword. You'd have been disappointed if I didn't give you a little show."

The Prince was speechless for a moment. He had forgotten to be conciliatory or even normally cautious. He stamped his foot. " 'Swinging that sword!' I was coming here to slay you! And I would have if you had fought fair. I slew a dragon just the other day."

"A fake dragon! I'm beginning to doubt you're even a real prince. Do you have any form of identification?"

The Prince sputtered and shook his fist at the dragon. "Of course I'm a real prince! And it may have been a fake dragon but at least it gave me a good fair fight. It didn't go flying off like a clumsy, overgrown bird.

It stood there and fought its best and died like all dragons should. . . ."

The dragon darted its head forward, gaped its jaws, and the Prince disappeared between them.

For a while the dragon sat there, enjoying the feel of the morning sun on its scales and ignoring the muffled sounds coming from inside its mouth. After these quieted, it sat awhile longer enjoying the stillness. Birdsong came from a nearby stand of trees and the ripple of water could be heard. Finally, after what seemed like a hundred years to at least one of those involved, the dragon opened its jaws and deposited a damp and chastened Prince on the ground.

"I'd like to rephrase some of my last statements," he said.

"No," said the dragon. "I think you're a little overexcited. Just sit there quietly and dry out while I talk.

"Now, there's a lot about this dragon-prince stuff that doesn't make much sense to me. Take those maidens, for instance. I mean, what was I supposed to do with a maiden? They were too small for a good meal and too ugly for romance. I tried to get some of them to do a little work around the cave, but they were too high-class to be much use. I carried them off anyway—it was expected of me. But the only thing they were good for was prince bait."

"When the princes rescued them, did the maidens automatically fall in love with them?" the Prince asked, a bit wistfully.

The dragon looked at him sadly. "No prince ever survived long enough to find out. And then I'd let the maidens go so they wouldn't clutter up the place. So what was the point of it all?"

"Adventure?" The Prince didn't sound too sure.

"Adventure. Yes, I guess it was, for me. It's always adventure for the winner. The princes might call it by another name, if they had the chance."

They sat in silence awhile. Things seemed different to the Prince than they had before . . . "Well," he laughed ruefully to himself, "before the dragon kissed me."

"I think you've come," said the dragon suddenly, "to try to steal back your sword. Perhaps even still to slay me with it, if you get the chance."

The Prince looked deeply hurt. "I'm sorry you think such a thing. Perhaps I should just go and not bother you any longer. You don't seem to like me."

The dragon raised a claw and scratched behind an ear. "I'm beginning another molt and I'm not fit for company these days. Not that I ever get much anyway." A couple of scales were dislodged by the scratching and crashed to the ground, narrowly missing the Prince. "I'm sorry. Now don't go off in a huff. Come in and have that tea."

So they went into the cave and the dragon heated a great cauldron of water with a breath or two and dumped in several tea plants to steep.

The Prince was staring into the corner of the cave. The dragon smiled, after its fashion.

"You're staring at my treasure," it purred.

The Prince gave a start. "No! Well, yes, but I was just noticing it doesn't look right. It's all golden, but the shapes are wrong. It's not coins and jewels and crowns and necklaces, it looks like . . ."

"Yes?"

"Well, junk. I'm sure I'm wrong!" he added quickly as he noticed spines and bristles rising up all over the dragon like hair on a cat's back.

"Junk," the dragon breathed, leaving a sulfurous tang in the air. "Go closer. Look carefully. Judge again."

The Prince moved forward, hesitantly, glancing with some longing at the sunlit cave entrance he was leaving farther behind. He reached the great heap of treasure and stood looking. Everything was vaguely familiar, yet made strange by the gold and jewels. He was startled to recognize an eggbeater with solid gold whisks and an emerald the size of a pigeon's egg for a handle.

"Did you ever sleep on gold? It is most uncomfortable. It is hard and lumpy and you mostly lie awake. When I was young, I spent those hard golden nights thinking of maidens and princes and treasure. As I got older, I thought about what on earth I could do with all that gold. So I taught myself to make things.

[27]

I needed no fire but my own, no bellows, no tools but claw and tail to forge whatever I wanted. I wasted a century on useless ornaments and swords and such things. Then one sleepless night I got the idea for a wonderful labor-saving device. It would carve, slice, dice, knead dough . . ."

The dragon began digging through the heap of golden objects, hunting excitedly. "I know it's here somewhere." It tossed aside glittering masses, all jewel encrusted. "Astrolabe, anemometer, potato peeler, barometer . . ."

The Prince retreated from the shower of priceless gadgets. The dragon forgot him in its excitement.

"You'll love this! It takes the place of knives, rolling pin, mortar and pestle . . ." It stopped for a moment and stared, bewildered, at an elaborate device. "What on earth was that? Oh, well." It tossed the thing aside and went back to digging. "Compass, sword, apple corer . . ."

With a clank, the Prince's sword landed at his feet. He looked at it. The dragon had been right. This was what he had come back for. A rush of contradictory thoughts and feelings swept through him, but his sword hand knew no doubts as it yearned toward its lost mate.

He looked at the dragon with its head stuck deep into its pile of treasures and its belly exposed. He grabbed the sword and threw himself forward into a double roll.

———

The King, the Queen, and the Princess were engaged in a royal audience. The King smiled benignly on the loyal vassals who sought his judgment. The Queen bestowed upon them her most beneficent expression. The Princess stared out a window.

Suddenly, there were approaching footfalls and the Prince ran into the Throne Room. The guards started forward from their niches on either side, saw who it was, and continued straight across the floor to the opposite niches.

The Prince stopped before the dais and hurled down two large green objects. He drew his sword and laid it atop them.

"Having slain the great and terrible dragon Ignispirus Magnus and endured hardship and privation, I claim the hand of the Princess, whom I awakened from enchanted sleep and had already slain a dragon to reach in the first place anyway."

Everyone was startled into silence. Then the Princess gave a little sigh. She pointed at the scales. "What are those things?"

"Scales hewn from the rocklike hide of the terrible dragon."

"Rocklike, eh? Yes, I think very much like rocks." The Princess sniffed.

The Prince drew himself up. "You don't believe me?"

"Now, now," said the King, "it's not that. We just

wonder why you didn't bring back the head as we had discussed."

"It was a very inconvenient journey as it was. You have no idea how awkward a dragon's head can be in difficult terrain."

"Well, a claw then."

"Dangerous to tote around. You could poke an eye out."

"Well, the ears then."

"Damaged in battle. Terrible, ragged, bloody things, not fit for ladies to see."

The Queen rolled her eyes up and nodded her agreement.

The Princess was staring deliberately out the window.

The King rubbed at his chin for a while. "Well, you see my problem here."

"No," said the Prince.

The King started at that. "Well," he said, "we still don't have proof of anything. Much talk of hundred-year sleeps and dead dragons but all we can put a finger on is some big green things."

"Scales! They're scales! Look at them! Did you ever see anything like them before? Doesn't that prove something?"

"Now, now, I daresay there are many things I've never seen, and almost none of them are dragon scales."

"Almost none," the Queen put in, smiling beatifi-
cally.

"Wasn't there anything else you could have
brought?" asked the King wistfully.

"Only kitchen gadgets," the Prince muttered.

"What?"

"Nothing, never mind."

The King sighed. "I think we shall have to find
some disinterested proof. Captain!"

The startled Captain marched quickly forward and
saluted tentatively. "My liege?"

"Take your men," the King began. Immediately
the Captain barked out a series of orders that brought
the guards tumbling into formation.

"Take your men!" the King repeated, shouting to
make himself heard over the din. "And seek out the
dragon's lair to be sure that . . ." The King stopped
as he realized he was shouting into an absolute stillness,
the guards having frozen in terror.

"To be sure that . . . ?" the Captain prompted
with a quaver in his voice.

"That the dragon is dead—which I am sure it is,"
the King added for the Prince's benefit. The guards
breathed easier. "And if it is not dead . . ." Silence.
". . . To finish the job yourselves."

The Captain began to call out commands and the
guards shaped up, wheeled about, and marched back
to their niches.

After some uncomfortable moments, the King called out, "Oh, Captain?"

The Captain marched smartly forward and saluted. "Sire!"

The King lowered his voice, just in case he was asking something foolish. "Why aren't you going?"

"Oh!" barked the Captain in surprise. "Did you mean right now?"

"Yes, now," ordered the King sternly.

"Don't bother," the Prince cut him off.

"So it's not dead!" the Princess snapped, eyes flashing.

"No, just offended. I stood it up for tea. I couldn't slay it. It took all my best moves just to make my escape with the scales. So there's no need to send your guards to . . ." The rest of his sentence was drowned out by the noise of the guardsmen dropping to their knees before the Prince and clapping their swords to their foreheads with such fervor that they all fell unconscious to the ground.

"Sorry," said the Prince. "If you'll excuse me, I have a dragon to apologize to. I was just beginning to learn from him that life is not the simple story I expected it to be, and then I forgot it all in a moment's excitement. I have failed at hero. Maybe I'll be better at doing odd jobs around the cave, if he'll let me." He turned on his heel and marched toward the door.

The Princess watched him go, then called out, "Wait!"

The Prince turned back and eyed her coldly.

"You're going to see the supposed dragon again?"

"Yes. So?"

The Princess started to say something, then sighed and lowered her eyes to the floor. "Nothing. Never mind."

The Prince looked at her. She was very sad and very beautiful. Suddenly he remembered his first sight of her and couldn't bear not to see those eyes again.

"Come on, then," he said.

She looked at him very hard, then around the Throne Room at all the appurtenances of royal life. Decisively, she jumped up and kissed her mother and father. "Perhaps he's not so bad after all," she said, tossing her coronet onto her chair as she ran out, pausing only to give the Prince a quick peck on the cheek.

The Prince looked back at the King, questioningly. "She's your problem now," said the King. The Prince bowed and started out. "By the authority of divine right, I pronounce you husband and wife," the King called after them, as an afterthought.

When the Prince was gone, the King contemplated his unconscious guardsmen and decided he liked them that way. He looked at his wife, who, having run out of suitable expressions, had fallen into a light sleep.

"Now *this* is the way a kingdom should run!" the King thought as he scrunched himself into a corner of his throne and closed his eyes.

The Growin'
of Paul Bunyan

THIS IS A STORY about how Paul Bunyan met up with Johnny Appleseed an' what come about because o' that meetin'. But it all got started because o' the problems Paul had with his boots one mornin'.

The hardest thing for ole Paul about gettin' started in the mornin' was puttin' on his boots. It wasn't so much the lacin' up that got him down (although when your bootlaces are exactly 8,621 feet an' four an' three quarters inches long, an' each one has to be special ordered from the Suwanee Steamship Cable Company in New York City, an' if because you're strong as ole Paul you tend to snap about two laces a week as a rule, then just tyin' your boots can be a bit of an irritation, too).

No, the hardest part o' puttin' on his boots was makin' sure he was the only one in 'em. Because, you see, they was so big an' warm that all the critters liked to homestead in 'em. So he'd have to shake 'em for nine or ten minutes just to get out the ordinary rattlesnakes an' polecats. Then he'd reach in an' feel around real careful for mountain lions an' wolf packs an' the occasional caribou migration. Fin'ly he'd wave his hand around real good to see if any hawks or eagles was huntin' game down around the instep. Then he could start the chore o' lacin'.

But ever' now an' then, no matter how careful he was, he'd miss a critter or two an' then he'd just have to put up with it. 'Cause once he had those laces all done up, it just wasn't worth the trouble to untie 'em all again.

So on this partic'lar day ole Paul is out o' sorts because of a moose that's got stuck down betwixt his toes. Paul's appetite is so spoiled he can't get down more than three hunnert pancakes an' about two an' a half hogs worth o' bacon afore he grabs up his ax an' takes off to soothe his ragged nerves in his usual way by shavin' a forest or two.

Well, the more his toes itch, the faster he chops; an' the faster he chops, the more his toes itch. Fin'ly, he can't stand it no more, so he sets down on a medium-size mountain an' undoes all 8,621 feet, four an' three quarters inches o' his right bootlace an' takes it off an' shakes it out for twenty minutes afore he remembers it was his left foot that was itchin'. So he gives a big sigh an' starts in on the other boot.

Fin'ly, both boots is off an' a slightly bruised moose is shakin' his head an' blinkin' his eyes an' staggerin' off betwixt the stumps. An' Paul has his first chance to take a deep breath an' have a look round. An' he's surprised, 'cause he can't see any trees anywheres, only stumps. So he gets up on a stump an' looks around an' he still can't see any standin' timber. He'd been so wrought up, he'd cleared all the way to the southern edge o' the big woods without noticin'.

Now this annoys Paul, 'cause he's too far from camp to get back for lunch, an' nothin' upsets him like missin' grub. An' when he's upset, the only thing to soothe him is choppin' trees, an' all the trees is down so that annoys him even worse.

There he sits, feelin' worse by the minute, with his stomach growlin' like a thunderstorm brewin' in the distance. An' then he notices somethin' way off at the horizon, out in the middle o' them dusty brown plains. All of a sudden there's somethin' green. As he watches, that green starts to spread in a line right across the middle of all that brown.

Now the only thing I ever heard tell of that was bigger than ole Paul hisself was ole Paul's curiosity. It was even bigger than his appetite. So quick as he can get his boots on, he's off to see what's happenin'. What he sees makes him stop dead in his tracks. 'Cause it's trees, apple trees growin' where nothin' but dirt ever growed before. A whole line of apple trees stretchin' in both directions as far as you can see.

It makes him feel so good he just has to take up his ax an' start choppin'. An' the more he chops, the better he feels. An' as he marches westward through all the flyin' splinters an' leaves an' applesauce, he sees that the trees is gettin' shorter until they're just saplin's, then green shoots, then just bare earth.

Paul stops short then an' leans on his ax handle to study the funny little man who turns around an' looks up at him. He's barefoot an' wears a gunnysack for clothes with a metal pot on his head for a hat. He looks up at Paul for a second, then he reaches in a big bulgy bag hangin' at his side an' takes out somethin' teeny-tiny, which he sticks in the ground. He gathers the dusty brown dirt around it an' pats it down. He stands up, an' out of a canvas waterbag he pours a little bit o' water on the spot. Then he just stands an' watches.

For a few seconds nothin' happens, then the tiniest littlest point o' green pokes out o' the dust an' sort o' twists around like it's lookin' for somethin'. All at once, it just stretches itself toward the sky an' pulls a saplin' up after it. An' it begins to branch an' to fill out an' its smooth green skin turns rough an' dark an' oozes sap. The branches creak an' groan an' stretch like a sleeper just wakin' up. Buds leaf out an' turn their damp green faces to the sun. An' the apples change from green to red an' swell like balloons full to bustin' with sweet cider.

The funny little man looks up an' smiles an' says, "My name's John Chapman, but folks call me Johnny Appleseed."

"Pleased to meet you," says Paul.

The little man points at his tree. "Mighty pretty sight, don't you think?"

"Sure is," says Paul, an' with a quick-as-a-wink flick o' his ax, he lays the tree out full length on the ground. "My name's Paul Bunyan."

The little man lifts his tin pot an' wipes his bald head while he stares at the tree lyin' there in the dirt. Then he squints up at Paul an' kneels down an' puts another seed in the ground. Paul smiles down at him while the tree grows up, then he lays it out by the first. The little man pops three seeds into the ground fast as can be. Paul lets 'em come up, then he lops all three with one easy stroke, backhand.

"You sure make 'em come up fast," says Paul, admirin'-like.

"It's a sort o' gift I was born with," says Johnny Appleseed. He looks at the five trees lyin' together. "You sure make 'em come down fast."

"It's a talent," says Paul, real humble. "I have to practice a lot."

They stand quiet awhile with Paul leanin' easy on

his ax an' Johnny lookin' back along the line o' fallen trees to the horizon. He lifts his tin pot again an' rubs even harder at his head. Then he looks up at Paul an' says, "It seems like we got somethin' of a philosophical difference here."

Paul considers that. "We both like trees," he says, real friendly.

"Yep," Johnny nods, "but I like 'em vertical an' you like 'em horizontal."

Paul agrees, but says he don't mind a man who holds a differin' opinion from his own, 'cause that's what makes America great. Johnny says, "Course you don't mind, 'cause when my opinion has finished differin' an' the dust settles, the trees is in the position you prefer. Anybody likes a fight that he always wins."

Paul allows he's sorry that Johnny's upset. "But loggin's what I do, an' a man's gotta do what he does. Besides, without my choppin' lumber, you couldn't build houses or stoke fires or pick your teeth."

"I don't live in a house an' I don't build fires an' when I want to clean my teeth I just eat an apple. Tell me, when all the trees are gone, what'll you cut down then?"

Paul laughs. "Why, there'll always be trees. Are you crazy or somethin'?"

"Yep," says Johnny, "crazy to be wastin' time an' lung power on you. I got to be off. I'm headin' for the Pacific Ocean an' I got a lot o' work to do on the way. So why don't you head north an' I'll head west an' our paths won't cross till they meet somewheres in China."

Paul feels a little hurt at this, but he starts off north, then stops to watch as Johnny takes off at a run, tossin' the seed out in front o' him, pressin' it down into the ground with his bare toes an' tricklin' a little water behind, all without breakin' stride. In a minute he's vanished at the head o' his long line of apple trees.

Now Paul has figured that Johnny hadn't really meant to offend him, but it was more in the nature of a challenge. An' Paul loves any kind of a challenge. So he sets down an' waits three days, figurin' he should give a fair head start to Johnny, who's a couple hunnert feet shorter'n he is. Then at dawn on the fourth day, he stands up an' stretches an' holds his ax out level a foot above the ground. When he starts to run, the trees drop down in a row as neat as the cross ties on a railroad line. In fact, when it came time to build the transcontinental railroad, they just laid the iron rails down on that long line o' apple trees an' saved theirselves many thousands o' dollars.

Anyways, Paul runs for two days an' two nights, an' when the sun's settin' on the third day, he sees water up ahead. There's Johnny Appleseed plantin' a last tree, then sittin' on a high bare bluff lookin' out over the Pacific Ocean. Paul finishes the last o' the trees an' swings the ax over his head with a whoop an' brings it down on the dirt, buryin' its head in the soil an' accident'ly creatin' the San Andreas Fault.

He mops his brow an' sits down beside Johnny with his feet danglin' way down into the ocean.

Starin' out at the orange sun, Johnny asks, "Are they all gone?" Paul looks back over his shoulder an' allows as how they are. Paul waits for Johnny to say somethin' else, but he just keeps starin', so Paul says, "It took you six days to plant 'em an' it took me only three days to chop 'em down. Pretty good, huh?"

Johnny looks up an' smiles sadly. "It's always easier to chop somethin' down than to make it grow." Then he goes back to starin'.

Now that rankles Paul. When he beats somebody fair an' square, he expects that someone to admit it like a man. "What's so hard about growin' a tree anyway?" he grumps. "You just stick it in the ground an' the seed does all the work."

Johnny reaches way down in the bottom o' his bag an' holds out a seed. "It's the last one," he says. "All the rest o' my dreams is so much kindlin' wood, so why don't you take this an' see if it's so easy to make it grow."

Paul hems an' haws, but he sees as how he has to make good on his word. So he takes the little bitty seed an' pushes it down in the ground with the tip o' one fingernail. He pats the soil around it real nice, like he seen Johnny do. Then he sits down to wait as the sun sets.

"I'm not as fast as you at this," Paul says, "but

you've had more practice. An' I'm sure my tree will be just as good as any o' yours."

"Not if it dies o' thirst," says Johnny's voice out o' the dark.

Paul hasn't thought about that. So when the moon comes up, he heads back to a stream he passed about two hunnert miles back. But he don't have nothin' to carry water in, so he scoops up a double handful an' runs as fast as he can with the water slippin' betwixt his fingers. When he gets back, he's got about two drops left.

"Guess I'll have to get more water," he says, a mite winded.

"Don't matter," says Johnny's voice, "if the rabbits get the seed."

An' there in the moonlight, Paul sees all the little cottontails hoppin' around an' scratchin' at the ground. Not wishin' to hurt any of 'em, he picks 'em up, one at a time, an' moves 'em away, but they keep hoppin' back. So, seein' as how he still needs water, he grabs 'em all up an' runs back to the stream, sets the rabbits down, grabs up the water, runs back, flicks two more drops on the spot, pushes away the new batch o' rabbits movin' in, an' tries to catch his breath.

"Just a little more water an' a few less rabbits an' it'll be fine," Paul says between gasps.

Out o' the dark comes Johnny's voice. "Don't matter, if the frost gets it."

Paul feels the cold ground an' he feels the moisture

freezin' on his hands. So he gets down on his knees an' he folds his hands around that little spot o' dirt an', gentle as he can, breathes his warm breath onto that tiny little seed. Time passes and the rabbits gather round to enjoy the warmth an' scratch their soft little backs up against those big callused hands. As the night wears on, Paul falls into a sleep, but his hands never stop cuppin' that little bit o' life.

Sometime long after moonset, the voice o' Johnny Appleseed comes driftin' soft out o' the dark an' says, "Nothin's enough if you don't care enough."

Paul wakes up with the sun. He sets up an' stretches an' for a minute he can't remember where he is. Then he looks down an' he gives a whoop. 'Cause he sees a little tiny bit o' green pokin' up through the grains o' dirt. "Hey, Johnny," he yells, "look at this!" But Johnny Appleseed is gone, slipped away in the night. Paul is upset for a minute, then he realizes he don't need to brag to anybody, that that little slip o' green is all the happiness he needs right now.

As the sun rises, he fetches more water an' shoos away the crows an' shields that shoot from the heat o' the sun. It grows taller an' straighter an' puts out buds an' unfurls its leaves. Paul carries in all the animals from the surroundin' countryside, coyotes an' sidewinders an' Gila monsters, an' sets 'em down in a circle to admire his tree growin' tall an' sturdy an' green.

Then Paul notices somethin'. He gets down on his hands an' knees an' looks close. It's a brown leaf. "That's not too serious," he thinks an' he shades it from the sun. Then he sees another brown leaf an' he runs back to get more water. When he gets back, the little saplin' is droopin' an' shrivelin'. He gets down an' breathes on it, but as he watches, the leaves drop off an' the twigs snap. "Help me, somebody," he cries out, "help me!" But there's no answer 'cept the rustlin' o' the critters as they slink away from him. An' while he looks down at the only thing he ever give birth to, it curls up an' dies.

For a second he just stands there, then he pounds his fists on the ground an' yells, "Johnny! Johnny! Why didn't you tell me how much it could hurt?"

He sets down an' he stares till the sun begins settin'. Then he jumps up an' says, "Only one thing's gonna make me feel better. I'm gonna cut me some timber! Maybe a whole forest if I can find one!" He reaches for his ax.

An' that's when he sees it. It stretches right up to the sky, with great green boughs covered with sweet-smellin' needles an' eagles nestin' in its heights. Johnny must have worked some o' his magic afore he left, 'cause when Paul struck it into the ground it wasn't nothin' but an ax. But now, in the light o' the settin' sun, it shines like a crimson column crowned in ever-green.

"I'll call it a redwood," says Paul, who knew now

he'd never want an ax again as long as there was such a tree.

So he waited for the cones with the seeds to form an' drop, an' he planted them all over the great Northwest an' nurtured them an' watched a great woodland spring up in their shelter. An' he never felled a tree again as long as he lived.

For years he worked, an' there are those who say you can still catch a glimpse o' him behind the highest mountains in the deepest woods. An' they say he's always smilin' when you see him.

'Cause Paul learned hisself somethin': A little man who chops somethin' down is still just a little man; but there's nobody bigger than a man who learns to grow.

The Fitting
of the Slipper

"PLEASE," implored the Prince, stepping back in some distress, "this is not fitting."

"Not yet, but it will in a minute," she muttered between clenched teeth.

"No, I mean it is not right."

She looked at the slipper in confusion for a moment. Then she took it off her right foot and began jamming it onto her left. "You might have said something sooner," she grumbled. "Your Highness," she added, remembering that she hoped to marry the Prince and must not snap at him until after the wedding.

She wore the daintiest little socklets, creamy white lawns with tiny red flowers strewn across them. They would have been enchanting but for the red that blossomed between the flowers as she tried to put herself in the royal shoe by any means available.

"I thank you for trying," the Prince began to say as he gestured for his Lord Chamberlain to retrieve the slipper.

She swung her foot away from him on the pretense of getting a better angle of entry. "No trouble, no trouble, just I've been on my feet all day and they're a bit swollen." She shoved a finger behind her heel and tried to force her way in.

The Prince stared, appalled. "This cannot go on," he sighed to his Lord Chamberlain, who knelt at the woman's feet.

"It can! It can!" she said, redoubling her efforts as she saw her chances slipping away. "It's almost on now." Four toes had found a lodging place and she seemed perfectly determined to abandon the last to make its own way in the world.

"No! No!" He pushed forward and grabbed the slipper from her. A smear of red appeared on his snowy-white garments. "I am on a mission of romance. I am seeking love and finding naught but greed and grotesque self-mutilation."

She pursed up her mouth like a prune and said, "Well, I never heard of shoe size being a sound basis for matrimony, but if Your Highness chooses to place his future on that footing, I don't suppose he can blame anyone for trying to cut a few corners."

"Silence, woman," the Lord Chamberlain snapped

automatically, but he looked as if he probably agreed with her.

"You do not understand," the Prince sighed. He stood openmouthed, as if looking for words, then shook his head. "You did not see her. You do not know the feeling of . . . Oh, what is the use?"

The Lord Chamberlain tried to take control. "If Your Highness will step outside, we have three more houses to visit in this street."

"No! No more! No more feet, no more blood, no more women who wish only to crush me beneath their heels! I cannot bear it!"

And with that he clutched the bloody slipper to his bosom and swept out the door.

Only it was the wrong door, and he found himself in a dark little hallway instead of on the street where the royal retinue waited. The door behind him started to open again and he knew it would be the Lord Chamberlain.

"You are not to open that door on pain of . . ." The only punishment he could think of at the moment was decapitation, and that seemed excessive. ". . . Of my severe displeasure," he finished, rather lamely. The door closed again and he was alone.

Before anything else could happen, he slipped down the hall and through another door. He was not sure where he was going or what he wanted, but he knew that he wanted to be away from what was behind him. He closed the door and dropped a bar into place.

He listened for any movement, but there was none. He was alone.

For a moment the Prince was so thrilled to be by himself that he paid no attention to his surroundings. He took a deep breath and listened. There was nothing. No one asking, "Is Your Highness ready to meet with your ministers?" No one imploring, "If Your Highness would only listen to my suit . . ." No one hinting, "Would Your Highness care to dine now?" Strange that it always sounded as if he were being asked his pleasure when in fact he was being told to do this or that right away. For being a Highness and a Majesty, he was always being bossed around by someone or other. The only time he was left alone was when he went to the bathroom. And even then it wasn't long before there would be a discreet knock and "Does Your Majesty wish to review the troops now?" Sometimes he would imagine himself replying, "Why, certainly, My Majesty always likes to review the troops with his pants around his ankles. It is a little hard to walk but it sets a good example for the recruits." But he knew he would never say anything remotely like that. And whenever he got that sort of thought, he would blush and say to himself, "This is not fitting." Then he would hurry up and be more obedient than ever.

For he knew he should be grateful for his wealth and position and that he owed it all to the love and goodwill of his people, and it was his responsibility and blah blah blah. Sometimes he felt that a very wicked Prince lived inside him and would leap out and take over if he gave it the least chance. But he had never given it that chance. Until now.

For a while he just listened to the quiet. It was dark and shadowy with only a little fire at the far end of the room and he could not see very much. But he could hear lots of lovely silence, and when he put out his hand he could feel the rough wood of the door. It felt wonderful to him, all uneven and knotted and slivery, and it squirmed with lovely deep-red shadows in the flicker of the fire. He could feel the glass slipper in his other hand. *That* was what he was used to in his life, everything smooth and silky and featureless. He held it up and looked at its crystal-line transparency, beautiful and perfect and boring. In sheer delight, he ran his hand across the rough landscape of the door.

And gave a howl as a big splinter slid into his palm.

He stuck the glass slipper under one arm and tried to ease the pain with his other hand. Then he froze and caught his breath again to listen.

Something had moved at the far end of the room. Near the fire, but in the shadows. In fact, one of the shadows itself.

He peered as hard as he could, but the harder he looked, the less he saw. When he moved his eyes, blue images of the fire danced in the dark. Even when he shut his eyes, the blue fire flitted about until he wasn't sure whether his eyes were open or closed.

He held his breath as tight as he could. But he noticed now that the breath he held was full of smells. They were kitchen smells, and to anyone who had grown up in a snug little cottage, they would have been comforting and comfortable smells. To someone like the Prince, though, who had grown up perfumed and scented and protected, they smelled like a wild beast in its lair.

He found himself wishing he had at least one of his guards or even a fawning courtier with him. Stories he had been told as a child came back to him, tales of witches and demons and unspeakable stews boiling on heathen hearths.

He had not thought of those stories in many years. They had been told him by an old peasant woman who had been his wet nurse when he was tiny. The infant Prince cried whenever she left him, and the Royal Nurse could not abide a squawling child, even if it was a Princeling. So the old woman had been allowed to stay until the child was old enough to learn that neither listening to silly stories nor crying was part of his responsibilities toward his people. One day he noticed he had not seen the old woman for a while. Eventually he forgot to notice when he never saw her again. He had outgrown her stories and her warm, soft hugs and her wet kisses.

Now he wondered how he had forgotten her. Her memory made the room a lovely warm haven again. Even the smells seemed to belong to her, and they comforted him like the low murmur of music from a distant place.

Suddenly a bent and twisted shadow stepped in front of the fire. The Prince gasped and grabbed for the door and gave out another howl when the splinter slid in a little deeper. The shadow pushed something into the fire. There was a little burst of light as a twig caught and then the shadow turned and thrust it at him, bright-blazing and shadow-twisting.

The Prince fell back against the door in absolute terror. He could see nothing past the light but a filthy hand, a coarse sleeve, and the dark bent shape beyond.

They were frozen like that for a moment of silence. Then the shape gave a low sigh in a rough, woman's voice. "Aaow. You am come then. I can't believe you really come."

There was something familiar about the voice, and the Prince straightened up to try to see. The shape abruptly dropped to its knees and the light lowered. "Your 'Ighness! I'm forgettin' me place! 'Ere is me all dirty an' bent over with scrubbin' an' stickin' the fire right in yer face like I 'ad any right at all. Please say yer fergivin' of me!"

The Prince stared down over the flame, at the wild, tangled hair and dirt-laden face, as if searching a dark thicket for a wounded boar. But instead of a ravening beast, that face held eyes bright and darting as twin harts startled by the hunt. He was still frightened, but it was different now. And she sounded somehow familiar. . . .

The silence stretched out, with him looking thoughtfully down at her and her looking up at him with a question and a hope that belied dirt and rags. Then he blinked and pulled himself together.

"I believe that you have the most awful grammar that I have ever heard," he finally said.

She didn't reply but slowly lowered her eyes from his.

"I do not mean that as an insult. It is actually quite interesting to me. Everyone makes such a point of being precisely correct with me, it is rather refreshing to hear someone jabbering away." She stiffened at that. "Well, I do not really mean 'jabbering,' just . . ."

Her eyes, which had veiled themselves, suddenly widened with concern. "Yer 'urt! Why din't you tell me?" She was staring at the blood on his clothes.

"Oh, that is not my blood," he said. "That came from this." He held out the slipper. She looked hard at the glass shoe and then raised eyes filled with some terrible emotion.

He found it impossible to meet those pain-filled eyes, so he held out his hand. "I do have a slight injury, however—a splinter from your door."

She took his hand without a word and led him to the fire. She pulled a rough chair close to it and seated him, respectfully but firmly. Then she knelt before him, studying his hand in the firelight. She glanced up to see that he was ready, then seized the splinter and pulled it out.

It actually hurt rather a lot, but he was determined not to show it. "Thank you, my good woman." He wasn't sure if she was a woman or a girl. Even close to the fire, the layers of dirt and ragged clothes hid her almost completely.

He started to rise, but she took his hand again and examined it. "Not all out," she pronounced, and hurried away to a dark corner where she sorted through the contents of a box with a great clanking of metal and wood.

"Actually, it feels much better and perhaps I will wait for the Court Surgeon." But she was back then with a long, sharp darning needle, which caught the light like a dagger. She thrust its point into the fire and waited silently for it to heat up. The Prince felt distinctly ill at ease.

There was a faint scraping in the hall outside and a low tap on the door. The voice of the Lord Chamberlain sounded deliberately unconcerned, as though pretending that nothing was out of the ordinary. "Is Your Majesty ready to proceed to the next house?"

The Prince looked nervously at the needle, which was beginning to glow red at its tip, and at the girl whose shoulders tightened at the voice. He wondered what the Lord Chamberlain would think if he knew he was closeted with a strange serving girl who was about to apply a red-hot point to the royal person. The thought almost made him giggle.

"Perhaps Your Highness does not realize the lateness . . ."

"My Highness is perfectly capable of telling time. Even now I am looking at a clock above the mantel. I shall come out when I am ready."

"Very good, Your Majesty." After a moment, the steps scraped away down the hall again.

She looked at him warily. "We got no clock in 'ere."

He looked abashed. "I know. It was a lie."

"You lie a lot, then, do ya?"

"Never! I just . . . It wasn't me, it was . . ."

"Was what?"

Something made him blurt it out before he could think. "The Wicked Prince who lives inside me and tries to get out." He held his breath. He had never told anyone about the Wicked Prince.

She didn't laugh. "The Wicked Prince 'oo tries to get out. Well, I guess 'e succeeded this time, din't 'e? Don't seem to 'ave done much damage. Maybe you should let 'im out more often. Maybe 'e woun't be so wicked if 'e just got a breath o' fresh air every onc't in a while." She smiled. And her smile cut right through the dirt like a spray of clear, crisp spring water and made him smile back.

"Let's see if we can't cut 'im some air 'oles right

now." She wiped the glowing needle on a rag and brandished it in the air with a piratical grin.

The Prince lost his smile. "Perhaps I should be going. There is a great deal of . . ."

She didn't answer, but knelt before him, grabbed his hand, and turned her back to him so that his arm was immobilized under her own, pressed against her side. It took only a moment, she was so quick, and he was left with the curious feeling of being completely defenseless and completely protected at the same time. She plunged the needle in swiftly and deftly. He tried not to think of the pain, and after a moment he didn't. His face was very close to her shoulder and all along the inside of his arm he was touching her. He could feel roundness and softness beneath the coarse fabrics. He could smell her smell, which was the scent that rises from under the earth after rainfall. And in the play of the firelight on her cheek he felt he could see beneath the dirt to some kind of shining essence that . . .

"I said, 'All finished.' "

He realized it was not the first time she had spoken. Yet she had not moved from where he half leaned against her, just waited for his pleasure. He sat back, embarrassed, and she turned and seated herself on the floor beside the fire.

"Not too bad? Yer 'and," she added when he showed no sign of comprehension.

"Oh! Oh, that. Fine. No pain at all. I am sorry that I am a little dreamy, but I was thinking of my old Nurse Reba. You make me think of her."

"Well, I don't know if I want to remind you of any old nurse."

"Not that you are old. I mean, I do not know if you are old. I mean, what is your name?"

She smiled to show that there was no offense. "Ella, Yer 'Ighness."

"Ella," he repeated. "A good . . . plain name. Fitting for a . . ."

"A good, plain girl?" she suggested.

"A good and faithful servant," he finished, trying to make it sound like a hearty compliment.

"Actually, I'm more in the line of poor relation than yer outright 'ouse'old servant."

"Ah, I see. A cousin of the house whose own family fell on hard times?"

She looked sadly at the walls around her. "This 'ouse is the 'ouse of me father."

The Prince couldn't take it in. "Your father? You are the daughter of this house? But this is a substantial house, so why are you . . ." He gestured mutely at their surroundings.

"Me mother died when I was a tiny one. Me father married agin an' 'ad two more daughters an' no more 'appiness afore 'e went to join me mother. Since then, this room 'as been me 'ome."

The Prince didn't know what to say. He felt deeply

ashamed that he had ever felt ill-treated in his royal position.

Ella felt his pity and hastened to add, "It 'asn't been as bad as 'ow it might seem. There's good in anything if you know where to look for it."

The Prince felt deeply uncomfortable. He decided it was time to return to his duties. He tried to find something cheerful to say. "I am quite sure you are right. And we thank you for your good service to your Prince. Now we must be going, for there is much of importance to be done."

He started for the door, but she was in front of him suddenly, eyes flashing. " 'Much of importance to be done.' More customers to try on, ya mean."

"What!" he exclaimed, drawing himself up into a state of outraged dignity. "How dare you judge your betters! You should remember your place!"

She fell instantly into a deep and clumsy curtsy. "Fergive me, Yer 'Ighness. I just want the best for you."

He was sorry for her, but determined to be dignified. "It is all right, my girl. It was really our fault for encouraging you in a way we should never have done. You have your Prince's gratitude and his kind thoughts."

She held her face in shadow and spoke low. "I just wanted you to know as 'ow I wasn't just what I seemed."

"Of course. Thank you and farewell." He strode to the door.

He was starting to lift the bar when he was stopped by a gentle rap at the door. He sighed resignedly and said, "Yes, my Lord Chamberlain?"

But it was the voice of the older woman who had greeted them at the door. "If Your Highness please, my other daughter is still waiting to try her fortune. Or if Your Highness wishes to stay by the fire awhile, I wonder if you might send Cinderella out so she can get to her chores."

The Prince looked at Ella. She had slunk back into the corner by the fire, merging into the shadows from which she had appeared. "Cinderella?" he called through the door. She raised her eyes to him then, but he could not read them in the dark.

"Yes," called back the woman. "Cinderella, our kitchen maid." She laughed. "Unless Your Highness was figuring to try the slipper on her as well."

The Prince hurled the bar into a corner and threw the door open. The woman fell into a deep curtsy at his wrathful expression. "Your Highness!" she gasped, not at all sure what she had done.

"Yes," he said after a moment. "You are quite right. Please rise." She did so, uncertainly. "It was my intention to try the fit of the slipper on all the ladies of respectable houses. So of course I shall try it on Ella. If there is time, I shall do the same for your other daughter."

The woman was speechless for a moment. "Ella! A lady?"

The Prince silenced her with a look. "She has treated us as a lady should treat her liege and as others have not. Await us without." He closed the door on the woman's white, startled face.

The Prince was furious but also delighted. It was the sort of thing the Wicked Prince would have urged him to and yet it seemed entirely in keeping with royal behavior. He might find a way to reconcile himself yet.

He turned to the shadow that was frozen by the fire. "All right, my girl, come over here and try this . . ." He stopped in surprise as she burst past him and tried to get out the door. He reached past her and slammed it.

"No, no!" she cried, fleeing into shadow. "Please, my Prince, don't make me do it!"

"Come, girl, do not be silly. Stop it! The sooner you do it, the sooner we are done. Come, that is a good girl."

She came to him slowly, unwillingly.

"If Yer 'Ighness insists . . ."

"I do. I command it."

"Then I must tell Yer 'Ighness somethin' afore I try on that shoe."

"What is it, girl?"

"It's my shoe."

The Prince blinked. "What?"

[65]

"It's my shoe. It fell off o' me when I was run-nin' . . ."

"What! Listen, girl, I am doing this out of the good-ness of my heart, and you are wasting my time. Just put your foot . . ."

" 'Me birthright for yer name,' " she said, and his breath caught in his throat. " 'If I stay another moment, I'll lose everything.' "

"How do you know that?" he gasped out. He grabbed her shoulders and shook her. "I have told no one except my father our last words to each other. How do you know them?"

She broke away from him and stood up proudly. "I know 'cause I was there!"

"But you . . . you . . . Look at you!"

She did not lower her eyes. "I clean up better than you'd expect."

"But you jabber away like a trained bird and dart about like a ferret! *She* spoke so precisely and moved with a stateliness that shamed the court!"

"You try 'avin' a conversation without usin' any 'H' words an' see 'ow precise you sound. An' if you want stateliness, just you 'op up onto a pair o' glass 'eels. Believe me, it's either stately or fall down in them things."

"Your gown! Your coach! Whence came they?"

"Well, whence they come was a friend o' mine. A person o' some power, I might add. An' don't ask to meet 'er, 'cause she operates on 'er own schedule and only shows up when I need 'er. An' she's the one as decides when that is, 'owever much me own opinion may disagree."

The Prince sat in the chair and began to rub his temples. "You do not understand what I am feeling. You cannot be the person. And yet you know things you could not know if you were not."

She stood behind him. "Why can't I be 'er?"

"You would not ask if you had seen her."

She began to rub his neck and shoulders. "Tell me about 'er."

He knew it was an unpardonable liberty, both her touch and her request, but the warmth and the shadowy darkness and the smells gave him a sense that ordinary rules had been suspended.

And her closeness.

"She was beauty beyond beauty. She moved like a spirit slipping the bonds of earth. She was light in my eyes and light in my arms. Each moment with her was molten gold, slipping away all the faster the harder I clutched to hold it. And with the stroke of twelve, the dream was broken and I fell back to earth. I do not expect you to understand."

She massaged his neck in silence while they stared into the fire. Her hands were rough and firm and knowing. He felt unfathomable content.

"You was so tall an' so 'andsome," she said from the darkness at his back. "When we danced, you 'eld me like a big dog with a egg in 'is mouth, like if you chose you could of crushed me in a second. Which you couldn't of, you know." And she gave his neck a teasing little slap. "But it was good to be treated fragile, even if I wasn't. You was so strong an' gentle. The music was playin' just for us, an' there was colors everywhere but I couldn't see nothin' but you. It was the best night I'll ever 'ave."

Her hands were still upon his shoulders. They waited in silence. Finally he spoke into the fire.

"If you feel that way, try on the slipper."

She let her hands drop. "No. You'd 'ave to marry me, an' that ain't what you want."

He turned in the chair and took her hands. "If the slipper fits, I want you."

"No. You don't want the slipper to fit nobody."

"That is mad. Why do you think I am going through the whole kingdom on my knees to every woman who wants to try her foot at winning a prince?"

She smiled. "It's actually yer Lord Chamberlain 'oo is on 'is knees."

"Figuratively on my knees. Why am I doing it? Tell me."

She shrugged. "To prove that no one is fitting." He started to object, but she silenced him. "You don't know that, but it's true. If you found 'er, she might turn out to be real.

"You felt sorry for me, but I feel sorry for you. Our night was like a beautiful dream for me, too, but I can wake up an' get on with it. I've got me little kitchen an' me work and I can be 'appy. And if me stepmother someday needs to make a connection with a rich 'ouse, she'll clean me up an' marry me off to some stupid, ugly oaf of a merchant's son. And I'll be 'appy 'cause I'll keep me 'ouse tidy an' me kitchen cozy and afore I goes to sleep, I'll think a secret thought about me Prince. And I'll sleep smilin'.

"But I can see *you* in twenty year. You'll be King an' they'll 'ave married you off to someone or other 'oo you only see at dinnertime. An' you'll drink too much wine an' shed a tear for what might 'ave been. An' you could 'ave been a good King, but you won't be, 'cause you won't want to get down an' dirty yourself in what's real an' common. You'll just be thinkin' about yer dream Princess. It'll be sad but it'll be better than if you found 'er an' married 'er an' discovered that 'er breath smelt bad in the mornin' just like real people."

He had sat down again as she talked. "What's wrong with wanting to live a dream?" he mused into the fire.

"In a dream, you got to play by its rules, an' there's more nightmares than sweet dreams in my experience. In real life, you got a chance to make yer own rules, especially if yer a prince to start off with." She stroked his hair. "Forget yer dream Princess. Be the King you can be. Think kindly of me now an' then, but don't let me 'old ya back. There's a beauty in what's real, too."

He sat silent a moment. She gave him a little push to get him moving. He stood and slowly moved to the door.

"Don't forget this." She picked up the slipper, saw it was stained, and dipped it in a bucket of water and dried it on her skirts. "Good as new. Drink me a toast out of it now and agin. Onc't a year. No more."

He nodded, took it, and turned to the door. He put his hand on the latch, then leaned his head against the rough wood. "I have to know," he said.

She gave a sigh. "Are ya sure?"

"Yes. As sure as I am of anything." He turned and knelt to place the slipper before her.

She started to lift her foot, then set it down. "There's one thing you ought to know afore I try it on."

"And that is?"

She rolled her eyes up for a minute, then looked back to him. "It may not fit."

From his kneeling position, he slowly slumped down into a sprawl on the floor. He cradled his head in his hands. "What are you doing to me?"

"Just tryin' to be honest with ya."

"But you knew our last words. It *must* have been you."

"Everybody in the kingdom knows your last words."

"That's impossible! I told no one but my father. He would never have repeated it to anyone."

"Yer sure nobody could 'ave over'eard?"

[70]

"There was no one else there!"

She counted off on her fingers. "Nobody 'cept for six guards, three table servants, two butlers an' one old falconer 'oo pretended 'e needed the King's advice about where to tie the pigeons for the next 'unt just so's 'e could 'ear the story for 'isself. Twelve people. Eleven versions of the story was all over the kingdom within twenty-four hours, an' the twelfth was a day late only 'cause one of the guards had laryngitis."

The Prince knit his brow. "I never noticed them."

She nodded. "You wouldn't 'ave paid them much mind."

"And that is how you knew what I said."

"No, I knew 'cause I was there. I'm just sayin' you 'aven't been quite as secret as you thought."

"Then why will the slipper not fit you?"

"Might not fit," she corrected. "Because it was got by magic. See, the person I mentioned 'oo got me me gown and all was me fairy godmother. She did the coach out of a punkin an' the 'orses out o' mice an' so on. So I don't know if me foot really fit in that glass shoe or if that was more of 'er doin'."

He rose from the floor and stood before her, looking deep into her eyes. He spoke softly.

"That is the most ridiculous story I have ever heard."

She nodded. "I guess I'd 'ave to agree with ya. Bein' true is no excuse for bein' ridiculous."

He laughed. "But I do not care." He thought a moment. "I don't care. I have felt more in the last hour with you than I have felt in all the rest of my life. Except for one night. And I can live with that one night as a golden, receding memory if I know that I can have every day with you. I love you, Cinderella."

She was troubled even as she felt the stirring of hope. "I don't like that name."

"But it is a part of your life and I must have it. I want to know all of you." He smiled with a contentment he had never known. "Marry me, Cinderella."

She burst into tears then. "No, no! It can't be. Look at me! Listen to me!"

"That's all I want to do. That and hold you forever." He longed to touch her, but he waited.

She dried her tears on a sleeve and tried to laugh, but it was a desperate sort of attempt. "I'll say yes, 'cause there's no way I could say no." He stepped toward her. "But first—I'll try on the slipper."

He stepped away from her and his brow was furrowed. "You don't have to do that. I don't care."

"Not now, maybe. But in five years or ten years, you'd start regrettin' it. An' regret is the only thing that love can't cure. So gimme that slipper. What's the worst that could 'appen?"

Hollow-eyed, he looked at her. "It might fit," he whispered.

She started at that, but looked him straight in the face and said, "Give it to me."

He set the slipper in front of her, then straightened. She touched her hand to his face and knelt to the fitting.

They stood, then, face to face. And there was so much hope and joy and fear and pain that neither one could have said which of them was feeling what.

"Look," she said.

He tried not to, but he couldn't help it.

The slipper didn't fit.

It didn't near fit.

He raised his eyes to hers and saw the hope in them change to a terrible fear.

"It isn't fitting," he said. "It is not fitting." She cringed. The Wicked Prince was out for good.

"It isn't fitting that a Princess dance on her wedding night in shoes that do not fit her."

Her face was crumpling. He could do nothing but go on.

"I shall have to summon the royal glassblower."

Her eyes flashed the question at him.

"To make you shoes that fit. The shoe must fit the foot. It's madness to try to make the foot fit the shoe."

She kicked it off and stepped close, and they stood a moment, savoring together the bittersweet of the last instant of aloneness they would ever know.

[73]

Then he swept her up into his arms, so strong yet gentle, as if he feared to crush her, which he couldn't have.

And the first step of all the many they took together smashed the glass slipper past all fitting.

The Working
of John Henry

JOHN HENRY got up that morning, just like every morning, and drank three cups of coal-black coffee, ate three stacks of flapjacks slathered down with golden butter and sorghum, and kissed his sweet wife Polly Ann twice good-bye and then came back to kiss her again.

He walked down to the railroad tracks and laid his hand on the rails. The steel was cold and sleeping, but he could feel way down to the frozen fire at its core, and that helped start the morning song in his heart. He walked along those tracks in the silver dew with the birds just waking up to sing and the sun showing just a bronze sliver over the hill. And John Henry felt like a newborn child. And just like when he *was* newborn, his hands curled to the shape of hammer grips and he needed only the heft of his sixteen-pounders to make him feel like a balanced man in the world.

When he got to where the tracks ended at the face of the mountain, he had got a rhythm in his feet and up through his body and only needed it in his hands to be complete. He nodded good morning to his team of six shakers. (Couldn't nobody hold steel for John Henry more than ten minutes at a time. Longer than that and grown men's hands began to tremble and their feet twitched and their teeth wobbled in their jaws and dropped out of their mouths.) He picked up his twin hammers and swung them once or twice to warm them to his grip and get the air to moving while the boys positioned the long steel rods for driving. Then he stepped to the rock face and began to play the song that only he could play, that only he could hear, the song that soothed the mountain and let men tunnel deep where they weren't welcome.

He'd played only the first few verses of his morning song when a call came from the boss man to come up to the shack.

There's no polite way to break off a tunnel song, so John Henry just played "Shave and a Haircut" for an ending and stalked off to the shack. Outside it was a little crowd gathered around a big heap of machinery. They were watching a man in stiff blue coveralls lay out cables and lines and tighten bolts and give little squirts of oil and generally play at working. The boss man was there, too, with his hands shoved in his back pockets, shifting from foot to foot while the blue man fussed at things.

"John Henry!" the boss man said, a trifle nervously, knowing the big black man didn't like to be called away from his hammering. "Look at this here. It's a thingy called a steam hammer. This man says it can outhammer ten men and work all day without a break."

The stiff blue man straightened up for a second and wiped off his hands that weren't dirty and said, "It can outdrill *twenty* men and work all day *and* all night. And you don't have to feed it or pay it or let it sleep. Just put water in the boiler and oil on the bearings and you can drill through a mountain like it was butter." He hunkered back down to his work.

The boss man looked at John Henry out of the corner of his eye. "Now what do you think of that?"

John Henry looked at the thing with all its bits and pieces and lines and cables twisting and turning. He looked down his arm to his hammer—the clean lines of flesh meeting wood meeting steel, black to brown to gray—then back at the steam hammer.

John Henry was a man who thought with his whole body. He felt the imagined pull and release of muscle and sinew and heard in his mind the rhythm of his hammers falling, *Tink TINK-ta-tee-ta*. "Looks complicated," was how it came out of his mouth.

The boss man thought about that, because whereas

most men said ten things for every one thought they had, he knew John Henry never said anything that he didn't exactly mean. And what he meant was worth listening to, if you could just manage to hear exactly what he was saying.

"Well, I guess a thing that complicated *is* liable to be trouble," he finally agreed, "but my boss says we got to give it a try and see what happens. He says to try it out against my best man, and I reckon that has to be you." John Henry nodded at that. He wasn't being boastful, there was just no point to lying. "So you head on back to the tunnel, and when we've got this thing all sorted out we'll come on over and see what's what. I figure a couple of hours will tell us what we need to know."

"A couple of hours? What are you, crazy?" It was a little man wearing a suit and a snap-brim hat. He was holding a pencil and a notebook in front of him like a magic wand and a hatful of rabbits. "We're looking a week of headlines right in the face here. At least! My editor would skin me alive if I let this one get away. We've got a slow news time going just now. There are no wars to set pen against sword and no droughts to irrigate with ink and no juicy famines to feed the presses, so our loyal readers need something to hold the advertisements apart. This is a great human-interest story. It'll stretch out easy for a week. It's a fortune in free publicity for you, and a great story for the public, God bless them: 'CAN MERE MAN MASTER MIGHTY MACHINE?' "

"This here is a reporter," the boss man said, as if he wasn't quite sure if this particular variety was poisonous. "My boss said we was to cooperate with him, that it's good for the railroad."

The blue man stood and wiped his dry brow with a white handkerchief. "Now I don't want you saying anything against my steam hammer. That wouldn't sit well with my district supervisor."

"Now don't you worry about a thing," the reporter said, and he waved his notebook in the air. " 'AMAZING INVENTION PAVES PATH TO PROGRESS!' reads just as well. It's all a matter of emphasis. A story like this can fit every which way if you know how to stretch it properly. We could even make it last a month!"

"A month!" The boss man shifted his feet nervously. "Why, in a month we'll be finished with the two Big Bend Tunnels and ready to move on down the line."

"Great! We'll see which one can finish the tunnel first. Make it a race! One month—night and day. Man against machine! Flesh against steel! Blood, sweat, and oil!"

The boss man looked at the little man like he wondered if this was a biting dog or just a yapper. Then he turned to John Henry. "Well, what do you think?"

John Henry looked at the reporter, who was stretching a wide smile across his face, too wide to look pleasant. *TINK-ta-tink Ta-ta Ta TINK-tink*. "Hammer-in's better than talkin'," he said.

The reporter stretched that too-big smile a little more. "It's settled then. The story will be in the paper tonight. The race starts tomorrow. Day and night to the far side of the mountain! May the better man win!" He stopped smiling, which was a relief, at least for John Henry. "Even if it's a machine."

John Henry went back to his hammering. He didn't think about the race. It wasn't until tomorrow.

———

John Henry got up the next morning and drank three cups of coal-black coffee and ate three plates of chalk-white biscuits drowned in slate-gray gravy and kissed his sweet wife Polly Ann good-bye and came back and kissed her twice more. Then he walked down to the railroad tracks and laid his hand on the rails. They weren't quite asleep this morning—a handcar had been by already.

That made him feel *TINK ta-tink*, "Race today." That was an unsettling thought, and it gave him a halting step as he walked up to the face of the mountain.

The boss man was already there, and the smiling man. The cook's helper was there in his apron, talking to a couple of farmers who had wandered over to see if they could sell some corn whiskey. And the blue man was there, a little less stiff today. He and a crew of three men were creeping around the machine, adjusting and tinkering. It chugged and shivered and some-

[82]

times gave an outright twitch that made them jump away a second before darting in again, like flies on a plow horse. The machine stood against the rock face with hoses trailing off to a big boiler covered with dials and pipes that stood about twenty feet off.

The smiling man ran up to John Henry and shoved a newspaper in his face. John Henry was feeling the need to heft his hammers to get his balance back, not some little bitty piece of paper, but he took it to be polite. He puzzled out the letters the way Polly Ann had taught him, at least the big letters at the top: MAN OR MACHINE: WHO WILL WIN?

" 'Before I let that steam hammer get me down,' " the reporter quoted from memory, " 'I'm gonna die with my hammer in my hand.' "

"Who said that?" asked the boss man, figuring as how he ought to fire anybody who said anything that stupid.

"Why, our man John Henry said it, in essence."

"It don't rightly sound like him. He usually talks a sight shorter than that."

"That's the power of the press. A man's inmost thoughts revealed without his having to speak a word."

"And a sight smarter than that, too."

He ignored that. "You're news now, Mr. Henry," the smile said between its teeth. "I've made you a pretty big man."

John Henry looked down at himself and couldn't see much difference, but he nodded politely and walked on. The boss man came and stood nearby as he swung his hammer. "Ready?" he asked, and John Henry nodded. "Ready?" he called to the blue man, who was posing for a picture next to his machine. There was a flash and a great cloud of smoke and his voice called out of it, "The steam hammer is always ready!"

"Well," said the boss man, "I guess you might as well start."

"Give it a lick for me," the cook's helper said as he headed off to sample the farmers' produce.

"The report of the starting pistol fired into the air was overwhelmed by the roar of the crowd," the reporter was writing in his magic notebook, "but the clangor of hammer and steam engine drowned even that." In fact, the rear legs of the steam hammer had collapsed, dropping it to the ground, where it spun in tight circles trying to take bites out of the human flies making desperate swoops at the off switch. And John Henry was standing still with his hand on the rock, feeling for a song he could play when he felt so off-balance. But the reporter had wandered off and, with the assistance of a little liquid inspiration, was transcribing the public's (or, more specifically, the cook's helper's) excitement at the start of the race.

Meantime, John Henry had started in to play "Twenty-seven Wagons Full of Cotton" in a tentative sort of way. And that dancy little tune began to lift his spirits and set his keel. But then the little men got their steam hammer tamed again and pounding full tilt at the face of the cliff. John Henry could hear it in between strokes and it was just noise, not a song. And it made him sad and it made the mountain feel fidgety and unsettled, so he shifted into "Mama, Hold My Hand," which was the calmingest song he knew to play.

Now the shakers who held steel for John Henry never knew he was playing songs, because he didn't sing out loud like some did, just let his hammers sing for him. But they could feel the shifts of rhythm and they could feel the moods he held. When the steels were sunk in sufficiently, the men would move a ways off while the powder man filled the holes and set the fuses and blasted away. Then they'd come back to a little more tunnel.

When lunchtime came, John Henry and his crew sat down to eat. But the steam hammer kept working, jarring and jolting away at the mountain. And John Henry had no appetite.

At day's end, John Henry laid down his hammers and started for home. The reporter caught him up.

"Where you going, John Henry?"

TINK-TA tink. "Polly Ann." That gave him his first smile of the day.

"Steam hammer's still working." John Henry knew that. He could hear the noise echoing out of the mountainside, like a big firecracker stuck in a tin can that never stopped going off. "Gonna work all night, they say, one-man shifts. They did quite a few feet today. How much do you reckon you did?"

John Henry looked a hard look at him and the little man held his notebook up like a shield. *Ta TINK tink.* "A day's worth," he said, and went home.

———

A week went by.

The first few days, there actually began to be some of the crowds that the reporter wrote about. People got their interest up about THE RACE OF THE CENTURY and WILL COGS AND WHEELS REPLACE FLESH AND BONE? They bought papers and they made the wagon trip out to look for themselves. The farmers set up little food stands where they sold fried chicken out front to the ladies and corn whiskey out back to the men. But when people could see how far ahead the steam hammer was, they generally lost interest. It was one thing to root for the underdog and another to spit against the wind.

The reporter had started out putting a little chart in the paper showing how far each tunnel had gotten, each bit of an inch representing ten feet. Then the steam hammer got way out in front, so the reporter changed the scale on John Henry's little picture to each bit represents five feet and that made it look more of a contest. But eventually even statistics begin to show the truth and, after a week, the sensation was dying down.

By Saturday night John Henry had done 90 feet, a steady 18 feet per day. By Sunday morning, the steam hammer was 144 feet into the mountain.

The reporter slipped into the church pew next to John Henry. "Why aren't you working?" he hissed. "How are we going to make a contest out of this if you take a day off whenever you please?"

John Henry looked at the teeth clenched in a snarl. He thought it looked better than the smile, at least more natural. *TINK-tink*. "Sunday," he said, and turned back to the preacher, who was just getting his second wind as the sermon tunneled past the hour mark.

Polly Ann looked around from the other side of John Henry and made a hushing noise at the reporter, who looked to her like he had no place in church except as a warning to backsliders.

"That's all very well," he whispered, "but I've got a story to write and you're letting me down. Listen!" The sound of the steam hammer floated down the valley and right through the windows of the church. It made a good accompaniment to the preacher's description of poor lost souls crying in the outer darkness. He had even brought in the steam hammer as a forerunner of the Antichrist, and the congregation, which stood to lose a lot of jobs if the steam hammer won, said "Amen!"

"That machine doesn't stop for Sunday," the reporter hissed, "it doesn't stop for night, it doesn't stop for lunch. That's why it'll be here when you're gone. Don't you care?"

John Henry wouldn't let that song play in his head. He had heard it try to get started before, and he knew it would drive out every other song if he let it. So he kept his peace and let his mind be soothed by the comfortable drone of the preacher's voice.

"Don't you care about the great race? Or what I wrote about you? You're letting all humanity down! No real man could just sit here listening to that infernal machine outside! You'd better be praying for a miracle, is all I can say!"

And at that moment, silence struck like a tornado. All the heads in the congregation whipped around to listen, and the preacher stopped midway between fire and brimstone. They had all got so used to the noise that they had stopped hearing it. Now, the silence rang in their ears like a clap of thunder. After a bit the noise started again, but then it stopped, sudden, with a crack. Nothing more. In the silence you could hear birds that must have been there all week, but couldn't be heard.

"Godbewithyouamen!" the preacher shouted, edging out the reporter by a nose in the dash to get outside and see. The whole congregation rushed down the valley, a Bible in every hand except for the one with a notebook.

When they got to the tunnels, the blue man was there in the coveralls, which had begun to look a little older every day. He was yelling at his man who was on shift when the thingummy broke. There was a spare and it had got put in right quick and it would have worked fine except it was stone cold and the machine was red hot, and before the two could split the difference, the new thingummy decided just to split.

It was the blue man himself who had put in the spare too quick and ruined it, because he wasn't too secure on the engineering side of his job. But he was very good on the yelling side, so that was what he was doing to make up. When he had fulfilled his responsibilities in that area, he sent the shift man to get a replacement part from the head office. In Cincinnati.

The reporter tore out the page of his notebook where he'd written "Man Meets His Match." At the top of the next he scribbled, "Pride Goeth Before a Fall."

———

The next week was sweet to John Henry. He played his old songs without steam accompaniment, and the mountain, which had felt more and more upset, began to calm itself.

Strangely enough, the crowd, which had dwindled, began to grow again. People who had gotten tired of the race now came to hear the music from the tunnel, which you couldn't rightly hear before. It became a favorite spot for a picnic. Ladies particularly liked to be there in the evening to cheer for John Henry when his day was done. He didn't see why anyone would cheer a man for doing his job, but he figured it was meant well, so he smiled and it made him feel even better on his way home to Polly Ann.

The reporter printed exciting stories of what he imagined was happening on the way to Cincinnati and made up charts that compared the depth of John Henry's tunnel with the distance to Cincinnati and back and made it look like a neck-and-neck race.

John Henry did twenty feet a day and went home every night with a happy ache in his muscles. Which Polly Ann soothed. So it was a sweet week and a quiet one. But John Henry knew he would never see its like again.

On Sunday night John Henry said to Polly Ann, "Tomorrow the steam hammer will start up again." When he was with her his thoughts didn't need to play in his head; he just opened up and they came right out.

She rubbed his shoulders. "I wish I could give you peace."

He smiled back at her. "You do. There's two things I care for—you and my work. After this week I'll still have you, so I guess I'm a happy man."

She gave him a little push. "I guess I don't never want to see a sad one, then. Why are you afraid for your work? You're the best that ever lifted a hammer, you know that."

"Yes," he said in perfect modesty. "But it looks like the days of my hammer are numbered and mine along with them. A man's only as good as the tool he holds."

Her eyes flashed at him, like fire springing up in coal. "And a tool's only as good as the arm that holds it!" she snapped. "Steam hammer can't ever know the mountain like you do, and any man don't know that is a fool, even if he is my husband!"

He looked at her in surprise. She never spoke to him like that. But he saw that all the anger in her eyes was love and she was only saying what he needed to hear. So he kissed her to show that he didn't take it amiss.

And then he kissed her to show he loved her back. And then he kissed her.

———

For the next week the two tunnels inched forward. John Henry played "Short Road Home" and thought of Polly Ann and did twenty-two feet a day, the best he'd ever done, which was of course the best any man had ever done. The steam hammer chugged round the clock and did its everyday twenty-four feet, but it had a long way to go to catch up. Come Saturday night, it was fifty-four feet behind. But when John Henry came in on Monday, after a day of rest and worship, it was only thirty feet behind.

There were big crowds every day now, and the rails were already hot when John Henry touched them in the morning. The railroad had put on special trains just to bring people from the big cities nearby. There were all kinds of food and souvenirs to buy, and copies of the newspaper stories signed by the reporter. Some people tried to get John Henry to pose for pictures with them. One man wanted him to swear it was Dr. Hekubah's Spiritous Liniment and Miraculous Muscle Relaxer that had made it possible. It all made John Henry feel real conspicuous and he was happy only when he was in the tunnel.

The boss man was waiting for John Henry at the tunnel and he took him off a ways where no one could bother them. He looked around nervously and said, "You've tunneled 342 feet so far. We figure it'll be 500 feet all together. Think you can keep up twenty-two feet a day?"

John Henry nodded.

"Good, good," the boss man said, and he looked way off down the valley, like he wished he was down there instead of where he was. "Now, I never was any good at arithmetic, but some of the men they worked it out and it looks like you'll beat the steam hammer if you keep going like you been doing . . . and if you don't take any days off. Like Sunday."

John Henry looked at him for a long time but no good answer rang in his head, so he went on back to the tunnel.

"I'm just trying to help!" the boss man called in after him.

That day John Henry couldn't keep any tune going for more than a few strokes. He couldn't find the

[92]

balance of his hammers. And he couldn't feel the balance of his life. Work was joy to him, but it was only part of the joy of his life. If to keep the joy of the hammer heft and swing he had to give up the joy of sitting proud with Polly Ann in her Sunday fineness and singing thanks to his Lord, then . . .

His shakers were scared of him. They'd never seen him like this. His blows had always been sure and regular and square on the rod. Today they came when the shakers didn't expect and fell off center and slid away and nearly caught their hands. And that made them hold more careful and ginger-like, ready to pull away. And that made the steel shakier and more strokes miss.

John Henry did sixteen feet, all day. Not much more than an ordinary man. By morning the steam hammer was just twenty-two feet behind.

The next day John Henry got back to eighteen feet. He did it mostly by shutting his ears to the ringing in his head. The songs he heard were too long and complicated to hammer, so he just bulled ahead through strength and habit. The steam hammer was sixteen feet behind.

Thursday, John Henry did twenty feet. He was twelve feet ahead and he was tiring.

Friday, John Henry hit hard rock.

He'd been hearing the different ring for a while, and he was afraid of what he thought it was. Then he swung a good stroke and the vibration of the rod made the shakers quiver like the twang of a mouth harp.

John Henry put his hand to the wall while he tapped, gentle-like, with his hammer. The hard rock ran deep and it ran right and left for a good ways. John Henry sighed and walked back a few feet and showed the shakers where to set the rods and began drilling off to the left, away from the straight line.

The boss man heard about this the next time they came out to let the powder man in. "John Henry! If you lose even a half day straight ahead, you can't possibly win!" John Henry shrugged at that. The boss man was upset because his job wasn't going to amount to much when his crew was just a bunch of machinery. That made him a little uncautious. "Rock too hard for you? Afraid you can't hammer through it?"

As soon as he said that, he felt worried, but John Henry just looked at him a little sad, then swung his eyes to his shakers, and the boss man knew what he meant. John Henry could drill through anything, but the shakers would be rattled to pieces by it.

"I'm sorry," he said, and meant it. "You do your job the best way you can, like always. I won't doubt you again." And he left him to it, even though he figured it was the end.

John Henry drilled about ten feet to the side until he could feel the good rock ahead. The next morning the steam hammer was six feet ahead of him. There was still ninety feet to go.

John Henry didn't think about that anymore. Polly Ann had looked at him hard the night before and said, "John Henry, you're a stranger to me." John Henry had just nodded. He was a stranger to himself. He hadn't spoken to anyone in three days.

He stopped thinking about winning or losing and just threw himself at his work. On Friday he did twenty-four feet, the best a man ever did, and he felt no joy.

Then the steam hammer hit hard rock at Foot 412.

The boss man offered some helpful advice to the blue man. "You're going to have to go around just like John Henry."

The blue man was offended by that. "We're not talking about some puny man here. This is a steam hammer! It goes through anything! You'll see why you and all your kind are finished!"

So the steam hammer kept straight ahead. And it drilled the hard rock. But John Henry could feel that the mountain didn't like it. It creaked and groaned and chewed at the drill bits.

Now, these drill bits were made special for the steam hammer, and the blue man had brought a good supply along with him, enough for a month extra. Until he hit the hard rock, and the bits, which were supposed to last a whole day each, now didn't even last an hour.

Saturday morning the blue man had to make a decision. His decision making was like his engineering, not nearly as solid as his yelling and his bragging.

So he was pacing back and forth in front of the tunnel when John Henry arrived. The steam hammer was still six feet ahead of John Henry, but there were only five spare drill bits left and no telling how much hard rock ahead. Those bits would last only five hours at this rate and there was still seventy feet to go.

When he saw John Henry, he started ranting and raving and John Henry stopped to admire that, because the blue man certainly did it better than anything else he'd seen him do. When he got the drift of what was happening, John Henry headed into the steam-hammer tunnel to see what was what.

The noise was terrible and the heat and the tangle of wires and tubes. He had to make signals at the shift man to shut the machine off. When the blue man realized where John Henry had gone, he ran after him, and the boss man followed, too. The reporter wasn't there because he had taken to doing most of his reporting from his hotel room in town.

"Get away from there!" the blue man yelled at John Henry when he saw him standing with his hand against the rock face.

"Settle down, you!" answered the boss man. "What do you think he's doing?"

"He shut down my steam hammer! He's trying to get ahead of us!"

"How's he gonna get ahead of you when he's right in the tunnel with you?"

[96]

There wasn't an answer to that, but he was about to answer anyhow when John Henry gave them a look that made them all quiet. And when it was silent all around him, John Henry put his hand back on the wall and gave a tap with his hammer. *TINK tink ta TINK tink.* "Two feet to good rock," he said.

The blue man looked at him hopefully for a minute. Two feet of hard rock would cost them two drill bits. They'd have three left to go seventy feet. They would make it! Unless . . . He squinted bitterly at John Henry, who watched him calmly, thinking that the man's limp, faded coveralls looked a hundred years old.

"Get out of my tunnel, you dirty liar!" the blue man yelled at him. "You want me to use up my last drill bits on the hard rock! You know there's more than two feet left!"

That made the boss man angry. "John Henry don't lie! And he don't make mistakes about what he knows. If he says there's two feet, there's two feet."

John Henry didn't stay to hear their argument. He went to his tunnel and used the burn of anger he felt to play twenty-five feet worth of "Far Over the Mountain." Anger felt better than nothing. And the blue man went back to Foot 412 and veered off to the right for eight feet to get around the hard rock.

When John Henry went to church that Sunday, and he did go to church, and the boss man didn't say a word against him, he was twenty-four feet ahead. When he came in on Monday morning, with forty-eight feet to go, they were stone-cold even.

But John Henry didn't care one way or the other. Because he had found his balance.

———

It had happened when John Henry was sitting in church with Polly Ann. His head felt empty without the hammer music it had lost. Then all of a sudden he thought, "Well, I lost my work songs. What does that leave me? Just my Polly Ann songs and my Jesus songs and my sunrise songs and my birds-in-the-morning songs and my Polly Ann songs and pancakes and syrup and bacon and dinner and evening and sleeping and day and night and the rest of the Polly Ann songs that I've hardly even started on. I guess that makes me a poor man."

And he laughed out loud, which was good timing because the preacher had just gotten to "He that dwelleth in heaven shall laugh them to scorn." And that laugh was such a good sound, and spoke so much to all the congregation who were worrying what would become of their jobs, that the preacher figured he couldn't do better. He gave an amen and wrapped it up at just two hours and a quarter. Sunday dinners had been coming early since the steam hammer arrived in town.

And Polly Ann looked at John Henry and recognized him again and that was the best thing.

So when John Henry came to work, he was happy and prepared for good or bad, whatever came down the road. And when he picked up his hammers, there was no song in his head, so he opened his mouth and made his own music.

His shakers nearly dropped the steel when they heard that big voice that had never strung more than six words together begin to sing "Can't No Hammer Get Me Down." But it was a good voice and it made them feel the song and they joined in, too, and most sang better than they ever knew they could.

The boss man came several times during the day to hear John Henry. "He always made the steel ring like music," he told the reporter, who had heard about this new development and had come to investigate. "Now he's doing the same for himself."

They were both there at the end of the day, when John Henry laid down his hammers and started for home.

"Eighteen feet today," the reporter told him. "Not as good as some other days."

"Every day's its own. Today was good for itself."

The reporter had never heard so much talk from John Henry. "The steam hammer will do twenty-four feet today. Tomorrow it'll do twenty-four feet. Then it'll be done. You'll lose unless you manage thirty feet tomorrow."

"That'll depend on tomorrow," John Henry said.

That night he ate the sweetest cornbread he'd ever tasted. And slept the deepest. And woke to the palest mist on the hills. And drank the blackest coffee and ate the heartiest bacon and eggs and kissed the deepest good-bye kiss. And came back for two more helpings of each.

He was four feet behind at the start of the day. And he sang songs so sweet and true that the crowds left the booths and picnics and stood quiet outside his tunnel and wished the steam hammer would break down so they could hear better.

At the end of the day the boss man and the reporter were there. "You can't quit now!" the reporter yelled, "you did twenty-six feet—there's only four feet to go! You're ten feet ahead but they'll pass you in the night and they'll win! Just two more hours' work will . . ."

The boss man shoved him out of the way. "Good day's work," he said to John Henry, who nodded and smiled and went home.

———

John Henry woke up the next morning to a dark, rainy day, but it was beautiful to him, because Polly Ann was there. "I guess I'll be home early. They won't be needing me anymore now that the steam-hammer tunnel is finished."

She looked over at him from the stove. "How does that make you feel?"

John Henry thought about it, then smiled. "Good.

A man needs to work, but I guess he can find it wherever he finds himself. Maybe I'll take up cooking."

"And maybe I'll give up eating!" said Polly Ann, and they both laughed out loud at that.

She sent him off with a kiss and a kiss and a kiss, and she smiled and waved and stood there and watched him go longer than usual, till she couldn't see him at all. Because she felt a fear in her heart that she couldn't name.

And she was right to be afraid.

When John Henry got to the tunnels, there was a lot of commotion and he figured it must be a celebration. Then he saw no one was smiling. The boss man came rushing out of the steam-hammer tunnel, and John Henry called to him, "What happened?"

"Cave-in!" he answered, and the word made John Henry shiver. The boss man gave directions to men who were bringing up barricades to keep everyone back from the mouth of the tunnel. John Henry made to go in, but the boss man stopped him.

"There's nothing you can do! He was just three feet from finishing, one more blast and he would have broke through, but the ceiling came down just this side of him, ten feet of solid rock. He's still alive because we heard him scratching at the rock. I sent in men with pickaxes, but I had to pull them out. The whole mountain's groaning. It could all go any second."

"Is the steam hammer still working?"

"No, the lines were all cut by the cave-in. I'm sending men to the other side, but it'll take them an hour to make it over the mountain, and there's no chance it'll hold that long."

John Henry put his hand on the rock by the tunnel. He could feel the creaking of the mountain's joints and he knew that it was about to give itself a good shake. Little rocks dropped and echoed in the tunnel like drips plunking into a cistern. It would all be gone in a few minutes. The mountain was fixing to heal itself.

The boss man had said there was nothing to be done, but he watched John Henry like he was hoping for a different answer.

"Who all's in there?" John Henry asked.

"Just Mr. Prothero. He didn't want to share it with any of his men when he actually broke through."

It was the first time John Henry had ever heard his name. "Prothero, huh? Is he wearing his old coveralls?"

The boss man looked at John Henry like he might be a little crazy. "No, he put on a brand-spanking-new pair today, so he'd look good in the photographs."

"Well," said John Henry, "we can't let him get his new coveralls dirty, now can we?" He picked up his two hammers and stepped past the barricades.

The boss man started to try and stop him, but his heart wasn't in it. He knew something had to be done, even if there was no hope. "Keep everyone back!"

he told his men; then he grabbed up an oil lamp and hurried in after John Henry.

It was like being in the hold of a tiny ship at sea, caught in the false calm just before the storm comes down. The lights were all out. The rocks groaned and the timbers bracing the ceiling creaked. There was only his oil lamp holding back the inky blackness and the weight of the mountain pressing down, ready to rush in like a wave no man could ride.

Every step was like diving into deeper water, such a lack of hope did the boss man feel. Finally he came to a standstill. He couldn't remember why he had followed John Henry in. There was no hope for Prothero, and John Henry was as good as dead. Why should he die, too?

Then he saw a flash of lightning in the black ahead of him and heard the clang of a mighty hammer blow. All of a sudden he heard John Henry's voice singing out the jolly words of "Yaller-Haired Gal." The sparks flew in time to that fast dance tune, and the mountain shuddered and cracked, and the boss man had a funny thought about how he'd saved the cost of digging a grave.

But the mountain didn't close down and it stopped its creaking and it . . . listened. Because nobody ever heard such a light, jaunty banjo tune played on such a sounding board. And when it seemed it had to slow down now, that no singer could keep such a pace going, the tune got faster and faster and the strokes came closer and closer together till it sounded almost like the steam hammer had learned to sing.

The boss man hurried up to where John Henry was making the rock dance to his tune. John Henry gave him a look and a smile, even though the sweat was pouring off him. He figured this was the last song he'd ever play and it was a good one.

And he was right, on both counts.

The boss man cleared the rubble from under John Henry's feet. As the boulders cracked, he shoved and pulled and wrestled them out of the way. In five minutes they were halfway through the ten feet of rockfall, and the mountain was still making up its mind.

John Henry's arms were moving in a blur. The light from the oil lamp made the sweat glisten on his body. His voice was beginning to crack now, like the rocks. But he didn't slow down.

Finally, John Henry's voice ended in a croak and there was no sound left in him. His hammers dropped in exhaustion. And the mountain decided to come down.

It started back at the tunnel entrance. There was a roar and the mouth just closed down like it was taking a good bite out of something. The people outside could hear that roar and that shake moving back into the mountain, swallowing timbers and lanterns and the only way out as it went.

The people inside heard it coming, like a railroad train determined to use that tunnel whether it was finished or not. "Good-bye, John Henry," said the boss man. "You were the best that ever was."

John Henry gave him a smile, then turned to the rockfall, took a deep breath, raised his hammers that weighed sixteen tons each, and played "Shave and a Haircut." And "two bits" broke through into empty space.

They shoved through the narrow opening to where Mr. Prothero was saying something they couldn't hear because of the closing of the tunnel racing toward them. John Henry shoved past the steam hammer and stepped to the rock face.

He put his hand on it and felt it carefully, running his fingertips over the cracks and crevices.

"Hurry!" the boss man yelled, but he couldn't even hear his own voice, the noise was so loud. He looked back and his knees trembled when he saw the rockfall roaring down the tunnel.

John Henry swung the hammers three times around his head and brought them down on the face of the rock.

And nothing happened.

The boss man was embarrassed to look at John Henry's failure, so he looked at Prothero's white, terrified face and felt bad that the last thing he'd ever see had to look as sorry as that.

As the rockfall swept into the little chamber and the ceiling began to drop, John Henry grabbed their arms, set his feet against the steam hammer and shoved backward against the wall. It fell outward, opening along faults that John Henry had split like a diamond cutter. As they passed through, they were caught up by the wave of rock and carried out and down. There was a great confusion of dust and noise and the pain of the little rocks grinding.

Then there was a lot of stillness and you could hear a pebble dropping here and there as the wave of rock settled down like a pond in a hollow and the ripples faded away.

The boss man stood up on his third try and looked around. The rock slide was like a tongue sticking out of the closed mouth of the mountain. There were no people on this side, just some cows looking on with mild curiosity. Prothero stood up next to him. He was shaking and trying to say something, but nothing was coming out.

The boss man looked around. "John Henry!" he called, but there was no answer.

"Why did he come for me?" Prothero managed to say, finally.

"He didn't want you to get your coveralls dirty."

Prothero looked down at the blue tatters he wore and couldn't think of anything to say.

Then, all of a sudden, a pile of rocks began to move and fall away and something that looked a lot like rock itself stood up and it was John Henry.

The boss man tried to think of words to say, but

there weren't any, so he just smiled and John Henry smiled right back. The boss man laughed. "Well, Mr. Prothero, it looks like John Henry got through the mountain first."

Prothero ground his teeth together. "Maybe so," he said, "but you know the railroad has already ordered more steam hammers, so it doesn't make any difference."

The boss man thought this was an awful rude thing to say in front of John Henry, but he knew it was true. "Maybe they'll change their mind after this morning's work."

"Just because your men didn't shore up the ceiling properly? No, the steam hammer is here to stay!"

The boss man knew it hadn't been his men's fault, but he figured that wouldn't make much difference. He looked at John Henry. He had an idea, but he was a little afraid to mention it. "I've got to tell you," he said, "my boss told me yesterday that the railroad has ordered three of those steam hammers and they're gonna lay off all the steel drivers. I'll find jobs for the rest." He looked at Prothero. "I figure it'll take most of them just to clean up the steam hammer's mistakes." Prothero snorted and turned away.

"But I'm worried about you, John Henry. I know what your hammer means to you, but if you could see your way clear to trying your hand at steam hammering, I guarantee you'll never lack for work. It's not music, but at least it's steel kissing rock, so no man could do it as well as you."

John Henry thought about that. Prothero looked like he was going to say something he might regret later, so the boss man accidentally knocked over a big rock on the little man's foot. While he hopped around some, John Henry smiled and said, "I guess I could learn to make noise for a living."

"How do we get back over the mountain?" asked Prothero, stepping carefully on the foot that the boss man had kindly kept him from putting in his mouth.

"I guess you're going to have to do a little climbing," the boss man said.

But John Henry walked along the face of the mountain and touched it with his hand. When he found what he wanted, he hauled off and gave it a great whack with his hammer, and a narrow crack split open. John Henry wriggled into the crack after he laid down his hammer. He would never pick it up again.

The boss man followed him through the crack, with Prothero behind. They found themselves in John Henry's tunnel, which had not been touched by the cave-in.

The boss man laughed. "How do you like that, Mr. Steam Hammer. John Henry finished both tunnels first!"

And the dusty blue man finally did try to call out

a "Thank you," but John Henry was already halfway back to Polly Ann.

Where he took the rest of the day off.

———

Now, you may wonder where the reporter was during all of this. Well, his stories had been such a success, he had been offered a job with a big New York newspaper. So he was halfway East by this time. When his train stopped for water, a wire was waiting from the correspondent (formerly cook's helper) he had left behind, telling him what had happened.

He opened his notebook and thought awhile. Everyone had loved his stories, except the people he was writing about, who never appreciated what he did for them. Now they had ruined the ending completely. John Henry learning to use the steam hammer! It was an outrage! It could only happen in real life. No one would ever believe it in a story.

So he wrote the story that *should* have happened. He gave it to the telegraph man to send out all over the country and he smiled that thing that passed for a smile. "I don't want any mistakes on this, particularly not in the last line. Send those words carefully—they'll make a man immortal," he told the key operator. "Even if he doesn't appreciate it," he finished to himself. And he boarded his train and went on to other stories.

The key operator was offended. He prided himself on his work and he didn't make mistakes. As he read the words, they sang in his head, *Dit dit da-DIT dit*, and he could feel them play in the muscles of forearm and hand.

He sent it all out exact, including the last line, which he read twice but couldn't see anything special to:

"He laid down his hammer and he died."

The Telling
of a Tale

"A H,' the giant sighed, 'there's nothing like a little music after a nice bit of toasted English. Sing!' he commanded, and the harp began to play monster hits from the Giant Top 40.

"He pushed his plate away and dabbed up the last few crumbs as he listened wistfully to songs that took him back to his youth, when he was merely huge. His face began to relax and he nodded off. He only knew two states of mind, anger and unconsciousness. Once he was asleep, he looked just like a baby would if you saw it from really close up, like half an inch or so."

My nephew Billy interrupted. "Didn't he have a beard?"

"Yes," I said, "a big, black, bushy beard." I wasn't bothered by his interruption. I tried to encourage any kind of response.

"Well, then, how could he look like a baby?"

"A baby with a cat sleeping on its face, of course." Billy nodded solemnly, acceptingly, as if that cleared up the problem.

"The harp stopped singing and looked around nervously when she heard a noise like a mouse creeping up the table leg. She was particularly high-strung, even for a harp. A hand and an arm appeared over the edge. And then a face and it was Jack, coming to steal her. So she gave a terrible scream and the giant woke up and blinked and said, 'Well, well, looks like I almost missed dessert.' His great hand closed around Jack before he could even make a move."

Billy listened critically but unemotionally. He had once been much more enthusiastic about the stories. But he had gotten older and less open to me, and now my sister, his mother, was making plans to move far away. This might be my last story, my last chance to give him the thing that I had been given. Looking at his noncommittal face, I was not sure he would take it or even recognize it if he had it. . . .

My Uncle Jack was the best storyteller I ever knew.

He told the old stories, but he made them his own. Dragons and fairies and elves and trolls spoke in new voices when he told their tales. Their patter was snappier, their riddles were actually funny instead of just annoying, and the action sequences, which were staged all over my bedroom, were pure Hollywood. They were the same old stories, but they were reflected in the fun house mirror that was my Uncle Jack. When it came my time to tell them, I would try to make them just like his, but they were always different, for better or worse. A tale always tells on the teller.

I loved when he came to visit, which was only one weekend every few months. As far as I was concerned, he could move in with us any day he wanted. After all, he didn't have a wife or kids of his own. But now and then was all my parents could take.

Uncle Jack was a practical joker.

He introduced me to the whoopee cushion, the squirting telephone, and the plastic throw up. I always fell for them. And I loved them. I was normally a rather serious child, quiet, with that passive quality often mistaken for good manners, and given to daydreaming. Only Uncle Jack and his jokes could loose the giggling anarchist who lurked just beneath the surface.

I often tried to get revenge, to play tricks on him. It looked so easy when he did it. But I never got the knack.

My mother tolerated Uncle Jack because, in spite of the jokes, he had "his good qualities." I could never imagine what could be a better quality than the ability to seduce one so casually into paroxysms of embarrassment and glee.

Whenever he came to visit, I would spend the day on tenterhooks, waiting for the inevitable humiliation. I giggled when he walked into the room. I jumped at a casual gesture. "Stop wiggling!" my mother would implore at the table. Uncle Jack would look at me now and then as if I were the strangest specimen he had ever seen and he couldn't imagine why I was acting this way. He would talk seriously to my parents about world problems and union affairs. I would begin to wonder if my mind had snapped, if my memory had played some trick on me. This man was obviously a typical boring grown-up, not the mad trickster whom I remembered. My breathing would get heavier, and tears of disappointment and bewilderment would start. Then I would put sugar into my iced tea and it would foam up like shaving cream, over the sides of the glass, wetting the tablecloth and everything around it, making everyone scramble to pull things out of the way while Uncle Jack asked my parents if they had ever seriously considered having me committed, he knew a judge who could handle all the paperwork. But he was smiling at me, so the world was all right. "Oh, Jack," my mother would say in a disappointed sort of way, and he'd shrug and wink at me.

My sister was never amused. She was younger, but very judgmental, very sure of what was proper behavior. Genius is seldom appreciated at the dinner table.

But that particular, delicious combination of dread and worship that I felt for him was for the daytime only. When I fell, exhausted, into my bed after a day of alarums, he would come sit by me and he was no longer the joker. He became the teller of tales, and I trusted him with my life.

You must be very careful whom you trust to talk you to the threshold of dreams, for terrible things can happen there if you are ill-prepared. The thoughtless remark can breed monsters in the dark.

There were no tricks, no joy buzzers in his stories. They were as real as could be, because he didn't make them up, he just told what happened. Stories in books were make-believe, but Uncle Jack's stories were true accounts, like newspaper articles from the *Never-Never Land Gazette*. "Just the facts, ma'am," he used to say. And he told his stories like memories of old friends, a little bit differently each time, but no less true to who they were and what they did.

When I told the stories, years later, they were different, too, but they always took me back to my blue flannel pajamas, and I could always hear Uncle Jack's voice in my ear. The telling of a tale links you with everyone who has told it before. There are no new tales, only new tellers, telling in their own way, and if you listen closely you can hear the voice of everyone who ever told the tale.

I only realized the greatness of Uncle Jack's gift when I became a writer and had to face the terrible blankness of an empty page. When the good stories, the real ones, come to you, you just open your mind to what the characters are doing and write as fast as you can. There's no feeling like that of a story flowing through you, scouring out the rust and garbage and letting you see clear to the heart of things for that little while. But a lot of the time it's not a real story with wings of its own, it's a jury-rigged contraption that you have to push every foot of the way to get it from "Once upon a time" to "happily ever after." Then you may think some liquid or chemical additives will help the thing run on its own. And if you grease your wheels enough, you can even fool yourself into thinking your gizmo runs smoother than any old flying horse.

Uncle Jack didn't need bottles or pills for inspiration—his stories came to him like breathing. But he suffered, I know now, with a terrible frustration. In another age, he would have led the shadow play around the fire at the mouth of the cave to celebrate the hunt and to give rest to the spirits of the slain. Or he would have sung the great songs to king and court amid the rich tapestries on high feast days. But in the world where we lived, he was a member of the electricians' union, with "a good job and a good wage," as he sometimes bitterly called it in conversation with my parents. And the only person in the whole world who knew of his wonderful, secret gift was a giggly little nephew who didn't even understand what he was hearing.

I remember the last story he told me.

I was very tired. That day, I had experienced snakes in the peanut-brittle can, red hots that made your spit look like blood, and a stick of gum with a mousetrap on it. All in all, a rewarding but tiring day. Also, I was getting older, reaching that age of little-kid sophistication when you lose belief in things or at least pretend to. The warmth of my bed and my inattention were lulling me into half dreams, when I suddenly realized he had stopped speaking. He had a puzzled expression on his face.

"What's wrong?" I asked, trying to wake up and stifle a yawn simultaneously.

"I don't think I can save him," he said with a sad little smile.

"Huh? Save who?" I sat up and tried to remember what he had been saying. I felt guilty that I had been falling asleep.

"Jack," he said, and for a second I thought he meant himself and I didn't know what to say. Then I remembered that he was telling me "Jack and the Beanstalk." I had loved the story when I was younger. I'd make him demonstrate the great, earth-shaking steps of the giant and his basso-profundo *Fee-fie-fo-fum*s. Now I was at an age when spy movies and TV shoot-'em-ups were beginning to hold more interest for me.

"I don't think Jack is going to make it," he said. "I think he's going to die."

Now that was a terrible thing to say to a child. He had always treated me like an equal, but we both knew who was the grown-up here, whose responsibility it was to see that things turned out right. I can only think he said it because he knew it was his last chance with me, because he had some suspicion, some jokerly sixth sense of the trap well laid, of what was going to happen to him. Within two weeks, there would be an accident, a car crumpled against an embankment. The hospital would call and my father would say, "They don't think Jack is going to make it."

"What do you mean?" I broke the unbearable silence, squirming under my covers. "He chops down the beanstalk, the giant falls, 'The End,' that's that. What's the problem?"

Uncle Jack looked at me with a wry, sad smile that hurt me. "You weren't listening, were you? Well, that's okay—I guess Uncle Jack's stories have gotten a little too old-fashioned for a big kid like you."

"No! I was listening. I just have a short tension span." It was an old joke of ours. Uncle Jack had had to explain to me why my parents had been upset by my teacher's comments, which I had taken to be obscure references to suspension bridges.

Uncle Jack laughed at that and I felt relieved. "Anyway," he said, "the harp screamed too early, the giant caught him before he could even get out of the castle. He's going to carry him into the kitchen and . . ." He stopped.

"And what?" I asked desperately, wide-awake now.

"And grind his bones to make his bread." The picture that familiar phrase conjured was suddenly terribly vivid. I had to fight a cold shiver.

"You've told this story before. Jack always wins. Don't worry."

Uncle Jack looked at me thoughtfully. "Things change. Just because it always happened before doesn't mean it will again. It's different this time. They're acting different. I'm worried about what's going to happen."

"Just go on with it. I'm sure it will be all right," I said with all the grown-up pomposity I could muster.

Uncle Jack didn't look at all sure, but he gave it a try.

"The giant carefully put the harp back into her niche in the dining room, where she preened and rippled her strings and sang vain songs about her great courage. The giant listened for a moment and began to beat time against his thigh. This was inconvenient for Jack, who happened to be what the giant was beating time with. When Jack gave an accidental little whimper, the giant remembered him and stalked into the kitchen, where he tied Jack down on a chopping board soaked with terrible red stains.

" 'Fee fie fo fum,' he said, picking up a big wooden mallet made from an entire pine tree, 'I'll spill the blood of an Englishman. Since he's alive I'll bust his head and grind his bones to . . .'

"This really isn't working out," I said, as my Uncle Jack had many years before. "Can you give me a hand with it?"

My nephew Billy looked a little pale and shaky. He didn't know how to react to a grown-up asking him for help. I hated to dump this on him, but it was probably my last chance, if he was ever going to get it.

He tried to help me.

"How about if Jack pulls out a machine gun and blows the giant away?"

"They didn't have machine guns then."

"When?"

"Once upon a time."

"I guess he couldn't be hit by a truck then, either."

"Not in his kitchen."

"What about a knife or a bow and arrow?"

"Why not a small thermonuclear device?"

"Yeah! That sounds great!"

"No! Jack didn't bring anything with him. You can't change all the rules just because you're stuck. Sometimes you just have to stay stuck and take the consequences. That's something you have to learn as you get older." This was the first time I had ever pulled the when-you-grow-up routine on him. I remembered how that had made me feel when Uncle Jack had used it on me.

"What about *The Wizard of Oz*?" I had protested back then, somewhat resentfully.

"What do you mean?" Uncle Jack said.

"When Dorothy melts the Wicked Witch with a bucket of water."

"What about it?"

"Well, why does it work? Why does water make her melt? She has them absolutely trapped and then she gets water on her and melts. Dorothy might as well have pulled out a tommy gun for all the sense it makes."

Uncle Jack thought about it. "You're right," he said, finally, "that was a cheat. If somebody in a story doesn't act according to what he is or what he knows or what he learns, then he doesn't deserve to win."

"But that's not helping us with Jack," I finished in unison with my uncle, playing middleman in this conversation across time.

"He could suddenly wake up and it was all a dream!" said Billy, echoing my own feeble suggestion from the past.

Uncle Jack looked scornful. "Your uncle's tommy gun is sounding better all the time. Saying it was all a dream is saying that your problem wasn't really worth solving, that your story wasn't worth the telling. No, I'm afraid we're just going to have to let him die."

"No!" I protested, very upset at that. It seemed wrong just to abandon him that way. "There must be something he can do! Maybe he can talk to the giant and persuade him that he shouldn't eat him."

"Why shouldn't he?" Uncle Jack asked.

"Why shouldn't he, Billy?" I asked.

"Well, he could appeal to his humanitarian instincts, like the Red Cross does on TV commercials. He's the only support for his poor, widowed mother—that sort of thing."

Uncle Jack looked doubtful. "Well, it's worth a try, I suppose."

" 'Wait!' Jack called up to the giant, who was waggling the gigantic mallet back and forth above Jack's head, practicing his swing. 'Think of my poor, widowed mother who will be left all alone if you kill me.'

"The giant lowered the club. 'Who is your mother?' he asked with what might have been a catch in his voice and the start of a tear in his eye.

" 'She's the sweet little old white-haired lady who lives in the yellow house at the foot of the beanstalk, hard by where the road forks,' Jack blurted out, feeling a bit of hope stirring.

"The giant laughed uproariously at that, pounding his fist so that Jack and the cutting board bounced and teetered on the table's edge. Finally, the giant calmed down and wiped the tears from his eyes and said, 'Your mother is poor and widowed because I killed your father and stole all his treasures.' Then he laughed some more, obviously thinking this a wonderful joke."

"I guess we can rule out the humanitarian stuff," said Billy.

"That seems likely," said Uncle Jack.

"What about using secret knowledge to gain time," I asked, "like James Bond does with Goldfinger?"

"What secret knowledge?"

"Well, Jack knows where the money is and the hen that lays golden eggs that he took back from the giant. He could use that!"

"Well . . ."

"Try it, at least!" urged Billy.

Uncle Jack shrugged.

" 'Wait!' called Jack as the giant raised the mighty club high above his head. 'If you kill me, you'll never find where your money and your golden hen are!'

"The giant carefully put his club down, seated himself, and dropped his head into his hands. His shoulders shook with emotion. 'No, no,' he gasped. Jack hoped he had struck a nerve, but when the giant raised his head, Jack realized he was laughing again. ' "The yellow house at the foot of the beanstalk, hard by where the road forks?" Is that what I'll never find out if I kill you? Listen, kid, I'm gonna have to kill you just to keep from dropping dead laughing.' "

"I don't think this is working," said Uncle Jack.

"What about health reasons!" Billy exclaimed.

"What health reasons?" the giant grunted, suspicious, hefting his club again.

"Too much red meat!" A phrase overheard on TV.

The giant didn't laugh at that, but raised his club high. He was done talking.

"Just our luck not to get a vegetarian giant," remarked Uncle Jack. "I'm afraid it's all over for Jack."

"No! No!" I cried.

"Yes!" the giant shouted as he reached the top of his swing. I could see it tottering high above me like a mighty oak struck by lightning, hesitating before its crashing descent.

"Stop thinking of all the tricks you've seen on TV or in the movies and start thinking like Jack!" In the frenzy of the moment, I'm not sure if that is my voice or Uncle Jack's or someone else's before him.

What are the giant's weaknesses? Looking up at that great brutish face, the muscles bunched on massive arms like jungle creepers strangling tree trunks, you can't see anything that looks like weakness. What does he care about? Gold. He has gold, he will soon have more, thanks to us. Food, drink. We're going to provide that for him, too, in a more personal way. What else? Nothing else.

"Help me, Billy! Help yourself!" But your face is blank and pale and your mouth moves soundlessly as you look up at the terrible sight.

You didn't get it, we think. We couldn't give it to you.

The club begins its fall, slow, then faster, then singing through the air like a tornado, like wild music.

Music! The harp! He loves his harp!

"There is someone who sings sweeter than your harp!"

The club smashed down and buried itself in the cutting board with a great crash.

The merest fraction of an inch away from this crater, Jack lay in a sweat and trembled at what he would have been if the giant had not swerved at the last instant.

The giant leaned down and eyed him suspiciously. "No one sings sweeter than my harp."

"Muh muh muh," Jack attempted, then swallowed twice and tried it again. "My mother does."

"Bah!" the giant shouted, and he began tugging at the club to loosen it for another swing. "Sentimental nonsense!"

"No! No!" I yelled.

There was a gentle tap at the door and my mother's voice called, "Everything all right in there?"

"Fine! Fine!" called Uncle Jack. "Go on!" he whispered to me.

"Who do you think taught your harp to sing before you stole her from my father?" I asked. "Think she learned on her own? Of course, she never learned to sing as well as my mother, but she's all right, I suppose, if you like second best."

The giant was lost in thought, not surprising since he had very seldom been there before. He scratched his head with the club.

"I don't think I believe you," he said, but looked as if he wanted to.

I shrugged as much as I could, wrapped up in ropes and sheets. "You could climb down and hear for yourself. You can always kill me afterward if I'm lying."

"Why don't I kill you now and then go hear for myself?"

"Because my mother will never sing again until I'm safe and sound. Then she'll sing for joy."

"But she wouldn't sing for me anyway." The giant looked away and there was a softness and a hesitancy in his voice. "She would be afraid of me. Everyone is."

"Not if you gave her a present to show you were a friend."

The giant was silent, looking away. Then he mumbled softly to himself. "I like music. It makes me . . . not angry for a little while." He turned back. "What present?"

"Oh, something for the house, not too expensive, how about one of your handkerchiefs? She could use it as a sheet."

The giant brightened at that and went back to the dining room to fetch a not-very-clean handkerchief from a drawer. "Perfect!" I exclaimed.

The giant quickly untied the ropes and carried Jack out of the house to the head of the beanstalk.

"You'll have to let me climb down on my own,"

Jack said. "If my mother sees you carrying me, she'll die on the spot."

"Don't you try anything!" the giant warned, shaking a finger the size of a log in Jack's face. "Remember I'll be right behind you and there's no way you can climb down faster than me."

Jack took the folded handkerchief under his arm and started down. As he cleared the bottom of the clouds, I could see only the soles of great boots descending above me. Far below was the little yellow house I never thought I'd see again.

"Now what?" asked Uncle Jack. "Can your mother really sing?"

"Not a note," I admitted.

"What will you do?"

"What Jack did," I said, unfolding my sheet and stepping to the edge of the bed. Grabbing just the corners of the sheet and hugging it to me, I jumped into space, hurtling downward faster and faster. The little yellow house and the green fields rushed up toward me. Far above, I heard the giant's startled exclamation and felt the wind as his hand swept by above my head in a desperate grab.

Flinging the sheet open, I heard a *Whoomp*! as it caught the breeze like a parachute, and I floated earthward. Looking up, I saw the giant climbing down as fast as he could. Looking down, I saw my mother's upturned face, frozen by the memory of the giant's last terrible visit.

"Get the ax!" I yelled. "Get the ax!"

She couldn't move—she could only stare. If she didn't get the ax, we were done for! I started to call again, but suddenly one of the sheet corners slipped from my hand. I began to fall, faster and faster, the sheet flapping like a broken wing in my face. This never happened before! I tried to grab it back but couldn't catch it without letting go of the other corners. The ground rushed up and I thought it was all over.

A slender arm reached from behind my shoulder, caught the corner and brought it back to my hand. *Whoomp*! and we were floating again.

I turned to look. It was the harp clinging to the sheet with me. But instead of the womanly figure I had seen before, it was a little girl in a pink dress with a flower at the collar.

"Thank you," I said, "but who are you and where did you come from?"

"I'm the giant's harp and I escaped by hiding in his handkerchief. My name is Alice. Would you like to smell my flower?"

"Very much," I said, proving that you can live a long time without learning anything at all.

She laughed immoderately as the flower squirted into my face, and then she knit her brow in a lovely parody of a scolding parent. "And just what are you doing in my story? You don't look like Jack."

"Your story?"

"My Grandpa Billy tells it just for me." She gestured

with her head below us. I looked down and saw a little old man standing beside my mother. He could have been my nephew Billy, grown old and bent. But he smiled up at me and his eyes sparkled and I wanted to shout for joy.

"I got it!" he called faintly and waved the ax at me.

But I knew he had gotten much more.

As we settled toward the ground, I said to Alice, "I told your grandpa this story when he was a little boy, just as he's telling it to you, just as you will tell it someday."

"You told him?" She thought hard. "But he said it was his uncle who told him the story, and he died a long, long time ago. It made him cry when he told me, and that made me cry, too."

I felt a chill at that. And a warmth. "Yes, I suppose I *have* died by now, but you can always find me here if you want me. As long as the tale is told, I shall never really be gone."

"Are you crying?"

"No." I brushed moisture from my cheek. "That's just the squirt from your flower. Sometimes it's hard to tell the difference. And now, Alice," I said, kissing her on the cheek as our feet touched down, "we've got to save Jack."

"Are you sure you're all right?" my mother called from the door.

"Fine now, Mother!" Jack ran to the base of the

beanstalk and began to chop like a madman. There was a twist and a snap and a crack and he grabbed his mother's hand and ran with her. The sun disappeared and a shadow grew across the land. The birds were silent in that terrible darkness, and it was unnaturally still.

Then the giant landed and the earth shook with the force of it.

The door swung open and my mother looked down at me, tangled in my sheets, lying on the floor. The night table and lamp were overturned from my giant fall. There were chips out of the bedstead where I had chopped at it with my baseball bat.

"What happened?" my mother gasped out.

"What do you think?" came the voice of Uncle Jack. And me. And Billy and Alice. And you whose names I will never know. "We all lived, happily, ever after. . . ."